CW00520330

A LI'
CHAT

First published in Great Britain in 2003 by
Paradise Press, BM Box 5700, London WClN 3XX.
Copyright © 2003 by Michael Harth

ISBN number 0-9525964-7-4
Cover design by Mike Lorenzini
Printed by Paradise Press

A LITTLE CHAT

Michael Harth

Paradise Press

Contents

CRUISING

Every so often I stop and take a look at myself, and I think 'What are you doing with your life, guy?' But it never makes any difference; in no time I'm back at the compulsive cruising, and the fact that it rarely comes up with the goods — or at any rate sufficient goods to make the operation seem to have been worthwhile when it's over — unfortunately does nothing towards curbing my addiction.

It was a good while ago that I decided I prefer cottaging to trying to pick up in bars or clubs, and such perhaps slightly more salubrious environments. Of course it took me quite a few years to find out that all the guff about romance and true love is really a form of brainwashing, and while it may work for some people, all it did for me was waste a lot of my time chasing after something I wouldn't have been able to handle if I'd found it.

Nowadays I'm just after physical satisfaction, and even so what I want is hard enough to get. The one advantage I can think of for the poor sods who happen to be heterosexual is that they all have a pretty clear idea of how and where a successful pursuit will end up, whereas with gays I've found it quite ridiculously necessary to check that they're interested in the same sort of destination as you are.

So far as I'm concerned sex means fucking, though of course I'm perfectly happy to stop at the odd lay-by before arriving at my ultimate destination. I'm slightly appalled at the number of gay men who don't share this attitude, and in my opinion it's due to their not having reached full sexual maturity. Of course some cite fear of The Plague as a reason for avoiding it, but I'm quite sure that's just an excuse.

When you're as matter-of-fact about what you want as I've learnt to be, purely physical criteria become pretty important, and that's where cottaging comes into its own. I have a quite pronounced preference for circumcised dicks, and it doesn't go down too well with the guy you're chatting up if you want to know whether he's had the op before you offer to take him back for a spot of activity. Whereas in a cottage, of course, the information is immediately available.

Other related information, such as the size and shape of your prospective's dick, is also there before your eyes, without the necessity for any potentially embarrassing questions, and subsidiary, but still important points, such as whether he seems likely to get a satisfactory hard-on can also be gleaned.

So most days, as soon as I've got back from the Hall Of Learning where I earn a fairly miserable pittance, I slip into a pair of jeans, get in the car, and drive off to one of my two or three favourite haunts. They're all some few miles from where I live, both to keep it off my own doorstep and also because I've learnt from thorough investigation that these particular ones are popular with the type of guy I'm most interested in.

Being a member of the effete middle-classes, at least by birth, it will probably come as no surprise to you that I go for rough trade, which I don't suppose I need to tell you actually refers to available members of the so-called working class. Of course I don't like real roughness at all: aggressive behaviour is definitely not my cup of tea. But I do find labouring types in general a lot more physically interesting, no doubt largely because they're

8

mostly much more comfortable with their animal nature than the rest of us.

In my time I've been with a lot of soi-disant bisexuals, many of them actually married. I'm dubious about the bisexual label, since I think the main reason they go in for heterosexual shenanigans is because they just accepted the loads of rubbish with which we're all clobbered right from birth, and so came to believe that men are naturally interested in women. In fact, close study has made it clear to me that most men are merely interested in sex, and other things being equal, they aren't be too particular where or how they get it: thus their ending up straight is, in most cases, just because they allow themselves to be trained into it. Of course there is a small percentage who only fancy the opposite sex from the start, but in my opinion that's just pervy.

I recognize, when I'm being exceptionally honest with myself, that there is some element of fetishism in my attraction to the R.T. afore-mentioned, since the less chat we go in for, the more of a turn-on I find it, and what I particularly enjoy is when any coupling is entirely silent, at least so far as verbal communication is concerned, and we part without having exchanged a single word, not even goodbye or thanks. This is obviously fairly difficult to achieve if I take him back to my place or go back to his, but it has happened on a number of occasions up the Heath, when it gave me a real glow of satisfaction.

Unfortunately I've now moved rather too far away from Hampstead for it to be a practical trawling-ground unless I'm preparing to make a night of it, and in any case I do a lot of my cottaging in the daylight, since I've found that catching trade on their way home from work is a particularly good time, no doubt because for many of them it's a last stop before they have to return to the tedium of family life.

Even so, there are of course plenty of occasions when nothing manifests itself that you can seriously contemplate.. Though, as the hours while on, your standards gradually get lower and lower, I have to be very desperate indeed before I'm prepared to go with absolutely anything that offers. Being as human as anyone else at bottom, though some of my friends would be prepared to dispute that statement, it nonetheless does happen occasionally, even though I can't remember a single time when the resulting encounter wasn't some level of disastrous.

I recall the last occasion well. It had been lean pickings all along, with all that was on offer being guys that I'd either had before or couldn't work up any spark of interest in. After some time of this, I and another guy who was also on the hunt were reduced to eyeing each other up. We had been standing at different stalls, but eventually, by not too overt stages, we managed to so place ourselves that we were able to examine what each other was offering without making it too obvious what we were at.

He was neatly dressed in trousers and a jacket, which normally acts as a warning signal to me, and should have this time, but as the minutes sped by, and still nothing turned up that either of us could fancy even considering the current dearth, I began the process of rationalising the situation by reflecting that he was at least decently circumcised, with a quite sizeable dick, and so far as I could tell solidly built — at least there was no visible sign of superfluous flesh in places where it would have been less than welcome.

I have no doubt he was going through the same sort of mental process, but still it was a good twenty minutes further on that we finally decided to give up hope of anything more interesting arriving. First it was necessary to check that we wouldn't be bread and bread, as they say; then we got into our respective cars, and he followed mine back to my flat. One ray of light was that he didn't have that smooth middle-class accent; there was a trace of lower-caste origins in his voice, so that, even though he was obviously a white-collar man, I was able to feel that going with him wasn't a total betrayal of my principles.

I may remark that I have mixed feelings about the kind of social mobility he evidenced. Theoretically, as a convinced meritocrat, I whole-heartedly approve of such endeavour, but since sex-appeal for me lessens in direct proportion as guys climb the social ladder, I am in practice less than enthusiastic.

Even then all might have passed off sufficiently well, but unfortunately my own middle-class training surfaced when we got to my flat, so that I foolishly offered him a drink. Nor did he have the sense to refuse and say 'Shall we just get on with what we came here for?' so I ended up making him a cup of coffee, which of course led into chat.

By the time I came back with a couple of mugs, he had removed his jacket and shirt, a move I approved of, especially as it showed him to be quite interestingly muscular. I could see he must work out, something which I ought to do, but can't summon up the necessary will-power. But unfortunately, while I had been irritably manipulating mugs in the kitchen, he had also been wandering around, looking at the contents of my bookshelves.

'You've got some fairly weighty tomes there,' he commented with a trace of awe. 'Are you by any chance a college lecturer?'

'Just an ordinary common-or-garden secondary-school teacher,' I explained. But the fact that you read works of philosophy and anthropology doesn't exactly increase your standing as a stud, so that I wasn't best pleased at his remarking on it, which no doubt contributed to the fact that I perversely continued :'I read that sort of stuff as a relaxation after coping with the mind-numbing stupidity of my charges. It's not quite so bad when I'm with the A streams, but trying to fill the heads of the Bs and the Cs with notions that are well outside their proper intellectual station in life is not my idea of time well spent.'

'That's a very elitist attitude to adopt,' he exclaimed reprovingly.

Once I've scented blood, I'm quite unable to hold back, even on occasions like this, and so I went on 'I should hope so. The idea that everyone should have an academic education is utterly preposterous. I admit there is a case for teaching everyone the Three R's, or trying to, but to imagine that an academic education is suitable for the whole populace is democracy gone mad.'

He had gone quite pale with anger. 'I have never heard anything so completely fascist,' he spat angrily. 'If that's what you really believe, you have no business in the teaching profession.'

'I'm in the teaching profession because I'm very keen that the five per cent or so of the population whose abilities warrant it should have the best education possible,' I explained. 'The rest should be taught how to handle a spade, or where to place what on the factory bench, instead of which they're encouraged to believe that they have some actual intellectual capacity, and that their opinions are of some value.'

'The main reason I went into the profession was that I believe a good education is the right of every child,' he informed me sententiously.

I don't mix with my work colleagues much more than I have to, since twenty years in the profession has convinced me that so many of them are wet lefties with not enough brains to spread on a slice of bread-and-butter. It certainly didn't make me any keener on this guy — we hadn't exchanged names, so I never learnt what he was called — to find out he was in the same racket, but on the other hand I had by then got to quite fancying him, and was distinctly looking forward to getting into his pants. Nonetheless, I couldn't stop myself baiting him further, even as I could visualise my chances of a screw flying out of the window. There are times when I don't really understand my own behaviour, and this was one of them.

'This idea of rights is a complete nonsense,' I informed him. 'The only rights anyone has are those someone chooses to give him, or that he takes by force. Anything else is sentimental claptrap.'

He had obviously led a sheltered life, since he sat there as if he couldn't believe what he was hearing.

'Do you spout these ideas to your pupils?' he managed to ask eventually.

'I do sometimes explain to them how fortunate they are to come into contact with someone of my intellectual status, though I feel it my duty to also explain to them that they won't understand much of what I'm saying; their plebby little brains couldn't cope with it.'

'I simply cannot believe what I'm hearing,' he brought out, his eyes practically popping out of his head with the intellectual strain I was obviously imposing on him. 'You should have been sacked long ago. If I knew what school you were working at, I would feel it my duty to denounce you.'

'O come on, darling, don't be pompous,' I exclaimed in tones of mock protest. 'That's not a nice thing to say when we're just about to get rather intimate.'

'We are certainly not going to do anything of the sort,' he announced, picking up his shirt from where he had thrown it.

'O come on,' I cajoled, going up to him and running my hands over his arse in a proprietary fashion.

'Get your hands off,' he snapped, pushing them away. 'I wouldn't have sex with you if you were the last man on earth.'

'Don't be silly, babe,' I said. 'You told me a little earlier that you really fancied a good fucking. And I must say you look rather sexy when you get cross.'

Between trying to keep my hands at bay and putting his clothes back on, he got in quite a state, but nothing I could say would calm him down, and eventually he departed without even saying goodbye. I was sorry not to have got my screw: on the other hand I had thoroughly enjoyed our little exchange, and was sufficiently high to get a really good wank out of it.

I didn't see him again at that cottage for a couple of months, but when he did eventually turn up, he gave me a sheepish smile. He had obviously come to realize I'd been baiting him, and I rather imagine would have been prepared to give it another go. Unfortunately, so far as I was concerned, any excitement he might once have generated was a thing of the past.

THE AMBASSADOR

The alarm bell was ringing, which was at least a break from the monotony. I went in to turn it off and find out what had triggered it, and there was Melmoth, sitting at his piano, playing something that I could tell was by one of the natives from the fact that it made no sense to my ears, to all intents and purposes quite oblivious to the call of duty.

I let it ring a bit, just to see if he would take any notice, but I should have known not to waste my time. Eventually I went over and stopped it, then moved to where he was, and stood at attention where he couldn't fail to see me.

He ignored me as long as he could, but eventually he had to look up and acknowledge my existence.

'Well, what is it now, Captain?' he enquired petulantly.

'The alarm bell was sounding, sir,' I said, stating the obvious, since I've learnt that he particularly hates my sticking rigidly to protocol.

'From the fact that I can't hear it, I deduce that you must have switched it off, Captain,' he said superciliously. 'I'm sure the next steps are all laid out with military precision in your handbook, so you may as well get on with them.'

'The regulations also state that the prescribed action should be initiated by the highest-ranking officer present, sir,' I reminded him, my military training overcoming, as always, my disgust at the fact that such a clown should ever have been placed in a position of authority, even in a totally unimportant backwater like this one.

'I know you well enough by now to be quite sure that you will stick to the rule-book, Captain,' he said wearily. 'So there is really no need for me to get involved at all.'

As Ambassador-in-waiting, all he has to do is sit around and wait for the natives of this unprepossessing planet to manifest some signs that they have reached a sufficient level of development to be admitted as a probationary member of the Galactic Federation. Judging by what I have observed, that is not likely to occur during his term of office, so the job is practically a sinecure. And yet, on the extremely rare occasions when something does happen that requires our attention, he resents it, and gets quite bad-tempered. In my opinion, all officers of the state should be required to undergo a period of military training; then they might be able to exercise some self-discipline. Though I imagine Melmoth is one of the worst: if he isn't, I shudder to think of the dregs which our Foreign Office must be trawling.

Since it is right on the far edge of the galaxy, I feel quite sure the only reason we ever organised the development of intelligent life on this planet was that there is such a tiny percentage of planets capable of supporting humanoid life that it is necessary to try even the longest shots. But if the powers-that-be had any serious hopes of civilisation developing here, they would surely have sent someone more competent than Melmoth. He seems to me to possess absolutely none of the characteristics needed by an official representative of the Galactic Federation, apart from an ability to empathise with the natives. And this, I fear, he takes to practically pathological lengths.

The maintenance of a proper standard of health necessitates my organising sexual relief for myself at regular intervals, as laid down in our handbook of procedure. There being no alternative, I am perforce reduced to employing various of the natives for this purpose, but I never allow this to degenerate into social intercourse.

Melmoth, on the other hand, appears to feel none of my natural distaste for fraternising with what is, admittedly, a strain of the parent stock, but one so little developed that the natives still breed in the original primitive fashion, and thus have not yet eradicated the female from their society. And the most distasteful, of all the distasteful tasks Melmoth requires me to perform, is to line up some male for him far more frequently than I consider appropriate to his age and position.

Not only that, but I very much fear that he does rather more than merely use them for their intended purpose: he actually seems to enjoy their company, though I don't have the faintest notion what he and they can possibly have in common.

From some of the tales I heard during my time at military academy, this sort of posting can be quite a fun time, with the ambassadors allowing their staff to sow a few wild oats, in accordance with military tradition. It's just my luck that Melmoth, who otherwise takes very little interest in the day-to-day running of the embassy, has placed a blanket veto on any amusements of the sort.

The only time I've seen him really furious was when he caught me stirring up a minor fracas — nothing much, just a few hundred natives, and with the primitive weaponry at their disposal I doubt if more than a couple of dozen would have been killed; nevertheless I got the dressing-down of my life.

But I was telling you about this emergency — though the term is a gross exaggeration for the nearest we ever get here to something exciting. It is, of course, a fact that, as civilisations develop and come up with the necessary technology, they eventually become able to dispense with the messy, and basically rather preposterous, compromise that is heterosexual intercourse. It is only a short step from that achievement to eliminating the opposite sex altogether. Unfortunately, on a number of planets this has gone the wrong way, resulting in their being totally populated by females.

There is thus a rival Federation, composed of all the planets where this contingency has occurred, and of course they are as keen as we are to recruit new planets into their group. Many thousands of years ago a treaty was worked out, under which both sides agreed not to interfere with natural process, so that, although we both keep observers on all the primitive planets, they are not allowed to interfere. This doesn't mean that they don't, of course, as must be obvious to all but the terminally naïve, but that it has to be covert.

We also have one other function, foisted on us by the science lobby, who, so they say, are keenly interested in certain atavistic characteristics that appear, though only rarely, in a few of the more primitive peoples. So my duties occasionally involve the kidnapping of some unprepossessing specimen to hand him over to a mobile unit if there is one near enough, or even, very occasionally, shipping some specimen they consider specially interesting to the nearest Federation planet.

Of course, I'm just a simple soldier, and my opinion doesn't count, so I will content myself with remarking that I have not been able to observe anything outstanding about any of those I've been ordered to collect, so that I wouldn't be in the least surprised if it wasn't some sort of elaborate scam. Whatever is going on, the Flibbers, as the general populace refer to our opponents, try to get in before us, and on a couple of occasions I've been too late to collect some particular Earthling: they've obviously got to it before me.

The fact that our alarm had just rung meant that another subject had been identified, and as Melmoth was clearly not going to attend to what was properly his responsibility, I went over to the console and tuned in to see what the fuss was about. Very soon I had all the information up on screen, and this time the subject conveniently turned out to be living in London, England, where we are based, so that I wouldn't need to chase all over the place for him. I started reading aloud from the monitor, and when I came to his psychophysical rating, which of course is the only thing we're interested in, I couldn't help sounding surprised, since he was down as over seven hundred, the highest I'd ever heard of.

That did finally encourage Melmoth to amble over, and he stared at the screen for quite a while before tuning in to a full-length picture of the creature. Its attire was obviously put together entirely for effect — an effect which was entirely negative so far as I was concerned, but Melmoth appeared to be fascinated, watching its gyrations, which were both ridiculous and fairly obscene. At one moment Melmoth turned on the sound, but he switched it off again immediately: even he hasn't let his interest in their bodies lead him into a liking for their current 'pop' culture.

Then, while he was at the screen, a message came through. I immediately suspected that the Flibbers have a better tracking system than us, because Melmoth's opposite number, a stroppy creature named Penelope, showing the sort of efficiency that he so disgracefully lacks, had already presented herself to the object of our mutual interest as a record promoter, and arranged to audition him the very next morning.

I've often thought that it would save an awful lot of trouble if our respective Federations could agree to just take the Earthlings of the appropriate sex as they turn up and do away with the need for all this skulduggery. Unfortunately the primitives don't oblige us by alternating the sexes in conveniently equal numbers, added to which most of them turn out to be false alarms, so that, after a quick checkover, they're put back where they were taken from.

Anyway, for once Melmoth actually responded to a situation with some approximation to urgency, going into action more energetically than I'd seen for a long time. He arranged to take the place of the regular accompanist at the Studio where the audition was to be held, which was uncharacteristically bold for him. Of course we have electromagnetic means of disguising our features and even our build, but if she should have the standard kit with her, she would know at once what was going on, and then Melmoth could find himself in a tricky position.

There was no particular reason why she would be carrying it, so I suppose it was a reasonable gamble, but I think the main reason Melmoth elected to do it was that for most of his fifty years here he's been playing the local musical instrument they call piano, and rather fancies himself at it. Fair enough, he can play some of the local stuff reasonably well, as far as I can tell, but one thing I know for sure, he's out of sympathy with current styles in the area of popular music. I tried to tell him, tactfully, since he's rather sensitive in the area, that he wasn't up to it, but he brushed aside my remarks.

So then I suggested I ought to accompany him for reasons of security. But he overruled me, saying in his over-confident way that he had it all in hand. I was somewhat alarmed to find out Penelope had obviously tracked the specimen down before we had, but, when I wondered aloud if she had been bugging our monitoring system, Melmoth dropped something of a bombshell. He explained to me that he had been economising on resources by only monitoring Penelope's monitoring system, leaving it to her to perform the planet-wide sweeps that form part of our duty here.

I pointed out that by this method we would never come across any possible subjects that her checks might have missed, and also that this was how she had the chance to initiate action before we had even received the report.

But Melmoth explained that he had a simple solution to that one: he let her have some of the low-level types, so that she could think she was accomplishing something, but if anything really interesting turned up, he had them disposed of, adding 'As long as we prevent Penelope and her gang from getting hold of them, H.Q. will be satisfied.'

I protested that, considering how rare these types are, it seemed a terrible waste.

'You have to look at it in terms of the overall picture,' Melmoth explained patronisingly. 'This is one crummy little planet on the edge of the galaxy, about as far from civilisation as it's possible to be. Its inhabitants have not reached a sufficient stage of development for us to reveal our existence to them, and at the rate they're going it seems quite unlikely they ever will, so really what happens here is of minimal interest to GHQ.'

'I wasn't told any of this when I was assigned here,' I protested. 'I can't believe it's official policy.'

But Melmoth brushed aside my remarks in his usual sweeping manner with 'It's my official policy, and I've been applying it for the last couple of dozen years without any complaints from home, so I think we can assume I'm on the right track.'

'I don't like it,' I said, a bit feebly, because really what can one do against such colossal and misplaced arrogance?

'I feel bad about that, Captain,' Melmoth said with a sneer.

Fortunately at this point my military training took over, so I just said 'Yes, sir. May I ask what you plan to do about this current case, then, considering our opponents are aware of his existence?'

'I shall go along to this audition tomorrow, evaluate the situation, and then, if it seems necessary, make the usual arrangements,' he told me

'You mean have him killed?' I asked, rather shocked.

But Melmoth had no qualms. 'It's the easiest solution, and the most effective,' he assured me.

Though I knew it was quite useless, I had to voice my objections. 'It still seems to me to be a criminal waste,' I exclaimed. 'Not to mention that we're supposed to be a non-violent civilisation.'

Melmoth can be, and for that matter often is, very sententious, and on this occasion he explained loftily 'You can only maintain a non-violent civilisation by getting rid of any sources of possible violence. You know as well as I do that the Flibbers are spoiling for a fight, and it's only the certainty of being trounced that keeps them from starting one.'

I consider it quite improper for a senior official to use vulgar slang, but any remonstrance would fall on stony ground, so I just said 'I'm not convinced.'

With his usual arrogance, he brushed aside my objections, and went off on his own to the so-called audition, though to be fair he did return unscathed, and apparently without having been rumbled. I asked how it had gone, when he said airily 'It's all under control, Captain,' and disappeared into his quarters.

I controlled my impatience, something I've had plenty of practice at in this posting, but then, only a couple of hours later there was a ring at the door-bell. I hadn't been informed that we were expecting any visitors but, when I answered it, the uncouth young man whose picture I had seen earlier on the screen more or less brushed past me and said 'Well, where's Mr. Matropolos, then?'

I was about to deny the existence of any such person when Melmoth appeared, dressed in what he probably thought was appropriately casual gear, and greeted the intruder. Then he performed distinctly desultory introductions 'Chris, this is Lan. Lan, Chris.'

But Chris paid only the scantiest attention to me; he was too busy confronting Melmoth.

'You're not the rich generous gentleman who wants to take an interest in my career?' he exclaimed in tones of disgust.

'Certainly I am,' Melmoth bowed his head slightly in acknowledgement.

'But you're that crummy pianist from the Rehearsal Rooms,' Chris expostulated.

Melmoth smiled in a superior manner. 'Merely one of a hundred disguises,' he explained.

'I hope the others are more convincing,' Chris said grimly.

'It's sad that you're unable to recognise true musicianship when you meet it, but I won't hold it against you,' Melmoth said in soothing tones. 'Let us direct the conversation to something more profitable.'

'Such as what have you dragged me along here for?' Chris suggested.

'During our brief encounter this morning,' Melmoth explained, 'I was smitten by your manly charms, and felt I had to see more of you.'

Chris was quite obviously well used to being chatted up, and I suspect enjoyed it. Certainly he looked more relaxed as he offered 'You can take me to the nudist beach if you like. Then you can see all of me.'

'So far as that side of things is concerned,' Melmoth said, rather more primly than I would have thought in character, 'I'd rather be somewhere that I could handle you as well.'

'I can see you don't know the nudist beach,' Chris remarked, and went on 'But aren't you taking a lot for granted?'

'It has been my experience,' Melmoth explained without shame 'that the little my personal fascination can't gain for me, the rustle of crisp bank-notes will.'

'So how much are you offering?' Chris asked in business-like tones.

Melmoth was not in the least fazed by this sordidly commercial approach. 'I confess to cherishing a hope that your excellent natural judgement would decide that my personal fascination was strong enough on its own,' he said smoothly, but Chris was having none of it.

'On the contrary,' he riposted, 'I shall expect double the usual rate.'

'Don't I get a discount as an old acquaintance?' Melmoth asked

'That depends on how genuine is your declared interest in my career,' Chris said.

'Surely you don't doubt my sincerity?' Melmoth asked, in tones that to my ears at least were reeking with insincerity, and to which Chris replied 'I've known promises that lasted no longer than the first orgasm.'

'The young of three continents could testify to my sincerity,' Melmoth assured him.

'And yet none of them are here to do so,' Chris pointed out. 'You must admit that is a somewhat suspicious circumstance.'

While all this badinage was going on, I studied the two of them. I could in a way see what had caught Melmoth's attention: the Earthling had a certain crudely masculine appeal, while he exuded a degree of vitality unusual in my experience. Of course, he didn't interest me in the slightest: I prefer something rather more refined, but animal coarseness, I have observed before, does appeal to Melmoth. In fact, sometimes I wonder if there isn't an atavistic streak in him somewhere.

Anyway, it was obvious, from the way they were striking sparks off each other, where they were going to end up, so I excused myself, with a suitably pointed comment which they both totally ignored, and went to my quarters to further my understanding of native psychology, which I do by means of studying everyday life as reflected in their soap operas.

The next morning Melmoth was in the lounge, which is also our disguised operations room, rather earlier than I had expected. Bringing me up to date, he told me that Penelope had of course agreed to put Chris on her books, and had already arranged three gigs for him, the first of which was the coming Sunday, four days away. I said, 'Well, we'd better get on with it, then: there's no point in delaying things. Do you want me to attend to it?'

For once he seemed to be slightly embarrassed, and eventually informed me that he was putting off action till the morrow, since he had arranged for Chris to spend the coming night with him.

I looked at him a bit hard when he told me that, since Melmoth is the original Mr. One-Night-Stand. 'Isn't that really excessively cold-blooded?' I suggested. 'Spending a second night with him, getting him to think you're seriously interested, and then having him bumped off the next morning?'

Melmoth, of course, is a master of sophistry. 'You are looking at the matter from quite the wrong angle,' he informed me loftily. 'You should rather consider that his existence is going to culminate in a night of incredible pleasure, after which anything else could only be a pathetic anti-climax.'

'Including death?' I asked incredulously, but Melmoth was quite brazen.

'You talk as if I'm going to enjoy having him rubbed out,' he complained. 'It's a political necessity which I very much regret.'

'Nothing like so much as he will,' I couldn't refrain from commenting, but he chose not to reply to this.

But when I came in the next morning, I found him doodling on the piano in a rather desultory fashion.

'A spot languid this morning?' I suggested.

No, no, I'm fine,' Melmoth assured me. 'Just thoughtful.'

I decided to find out what was going on in his devious little mind. 'I think we ought to make our minds up now in what way our young friend is going to be disposed of, sir: then I can get on with the arrangements. Or have you seen to it already?' I asked blandly.

'Er, no, I haven't,' was all he could say.

He obviously wasn't keen to pursue the subject, so I cheerfully went on 'Every day we put it off increases the risk.'

'O, I don't know,' he excused himself. 'So long as we keep careful tabs on Penelope, we should be okay.'

I looked directly at him and asked 'Not getting squeamish in our old age, are we?

'No, no: I wouldn't say that,' he dithered. But then the door-bell went, and I answered it, fearing the worst. Sure enough, Chris came in, carrying a handcase, greeted us cursorily, and went straight through into Melmoth's quarters.

'Hey, what's this?' I asked, feeling that things were starting to get out of hand.

'Well, he asked me to give him some help rehearsing his act,' Melmoth explained, 'and I couldn't very well refuse.'

'He's moving in here for it?' I asked incredulously.

'Purely convenience,' Melmoth said airily, adding pointedly 'We shall be rehearsing shortly.' I was only too glad to remove myself from the scene of what would surely not only have been an awful noise, but would have been peppered with the endless bickering which it was apparent they both enjoyed.

Late the next morning, the phone rang while I was in the operations room, and the call was for Chris, if you please. I assuaged my irritation at the liberty with the thought that it wouldn't be for long, and called him on the intercom, since neither of them had so far made an appearance. Very soon I saw the light go out, which meant that the call had finished, and only a few minutes later Chris emerged, closely followed by Melmoth in semi-déshabille

Chris was explaining to Melmoth 'That was my recording company: the band want to go through my spot with me before the gig, and this evening is the only time they have free. But I should be back by eight at the latest.'

He was already walking out while Melmoth digested this piece of information, and though I knew it was a kind of emergency, still it was such a pleasure to see him caught short that I didn't interfere. To be fair, he recovered quickly, and before Chris disappeared asked him urgently 'Are you sure that's a good idea?'

'Of course it's a good idea' Chris retorted. 'The group needs to get to know my style, and I need to get to know theirs.'

Melmoth was still floundering. 'You don't think it would give your performance a sort of freshness if you came new to each other?' was the best he could come up with.

'It would be a shambles' Chris said very definitely. 'See you later.' And then he really was gone.

Melmoth looked at me and snapped 'Well, what are you waiting for? It might be a perfectly bona fide rehearsal, but we can't afford to take the chance. Go after him.'

'What do you want me to do?' I asked.

'Can't you use your initiative?' Melmoth snapped.

I pointed out to him with a certain degree of pleasure 'You only like me using my initiative when I have the same ideas as you. So I find it safer to check first.'

Melmoth is not really a man of action, and dislikes having to make that sort of decision, He hesitated for a moment, and then said irritably ' I suppose you'd better kidnap him and bring him back here.'

'How do you suggest I do that?' I enquired.

He was getting more and more impatient. 'Anyway you like. Haven't you ever kidnapped anybody before?

'I certainly haven't,' I said with spirit.

'What a deprived life you've led,' he remarked, getting back to his old sarcastic self. ' I don't know what they teach you at Military Academy these days. I think

I'd better come with you. Dial us a couple of disguises, will you?'

I went over to the machine bank, but before setting the parameters I hesitated, unsure what would be suitable.

'Fast!' Melmoth yelled impatiently.

'What sort of disguises?' I thought it better to ask.

'Can't you ever think for yourself?' he complained. 'Let me see — ah, I know, we'll be ambulance men. And lay on an ambulance, while you're at it.'

Then while I was dialling, getting armbands and so on from the machine, and passing one of each to him, he called out 'And make sure the ambulance has a siren, so we can dash through the traffic to the scene of the accident.'

If he were a suitable person to be in authority over others, he would explain his actions or decisions to his subordinates; then maybe he would be easier to work with. But he's far too arrogant for that; he expects you to follow the way his brain jumps from one idea to the other, and then gets cross when you can't. Of course, I'm quite inured to it by now, so I just asked patiently 'What accident?'

'Chris's accident,' he explained, as if it were obvious to a child of three.

'Has something happened to him already?' I was confused.

Melmoth snorted dismissively. 'You need to take a course in positive thinking.' he said. 'Why would we load him onto a stretcher if he hadn't had an accident?'

I was quite at a loss. 'But ..' I stammered.

'What do you think I'm taking this stun-gun for?' he asked rhetorically. 'Landscape-painting?'

'I still don't understand what you're ..' I started, but Melmoth interrupted with the threat 'If you don't shut up making silly noises, I shall do the driving.'

I shut up, and off we went.

I was slightly appalled, and perhaps just a little impressed, by the ruthlessness with which Melmoth knocked Chris out with one of our anaesthetic darts, and had him on a stretcher inside the ambulance before a crowd had time to gather. Soon we were speeding back with the siren blaring, I drove the van into our concealed garage, and shortly we were carrying Chris, still on the stretcher, into our rarely-used function room. Then Melmoth administered a sniff of the antidote while I untied him.

It took a few moments for him to gather his wits, then he sat up and protested 'Just what is all this about? Nobody's going to ransom me for a million pounds. You'd be lucky if you got a hundred.'

So I removed my disguise, and by the time I'd peeled off the moustache he was able to recognise me.

'You!' he yelled. 'Just what is all this performance about?'

Melmoth, who was in the act of removing the ghastly hat he had assumed, had quite recovered his usual aplomb. 'A tribute to your fatal fascination,' he explained. 'I realised that life would be meaningless without you as soon as you went out of the door.'

'Quite. So you commandeered an ambulance to bring me back,' Chris said sarcastically. 'Pull the other one.'

'You underestimate your importance to me,' Melmoth said.

'I assume there must actually be some reason for this charade,' Chris was not in the mood for persiflage. 'So perhaps you'd better come out with it.'

I thought I'd better try to soften the blow before Melmoth went totally over the top, so I warned him 'You wouldn't believe us.'

Then Melmoth took over. 'You see, I'm not really a pianist,' he started.

Chris couldn't resist such an opening and got in quickly with 'I knew that as soon as I heard you play.'

But for once Melmoth didn't rise, and eventually, between the two of us, we managed to explain the reasons for our actions to Chris, who didn't seem all that amazed, which fact I put down to a diet of rubbishy science-fiction films. By now I had realised that Melmoth wasn't going to be able to bring himself to have Chris killed, but that one decision seemed to close off all his other options, and he was still vacillating when his mind was made up for him. Penelope, having over-ridden our security procedures with an impunity which said there was something that badly needed looking into, sauntered in holding a weapon at the ready.

Neither of us noticed her at first: we were too busy trying to explain things to Chris, so she interrupted in a casual tone of voice with 'I'm sorry to have to break up such a delightful little gathering.'

Melmoth managed to retain his poise. 'To what do we owe the pleasure?' he asked.

'To your complacency and inefficiency, largely,' Penelope told him. 'Just what I would expect of those brought up in a masculine culture.'

'As you're waving a laser around, I suppose I shall have to endure the party political,' Melmoth riposted.

'O, you needn't be alarmed,' Penelope smiled. 'I shall be quite content with a spot of political action. I'm merely here to rescue my protégé from your sinister clutches.'

'You've picked a rather inopportune moment, just when I was beginning to get him to rock a bit,' Chris complained.

'You'll have every opportunity to indulge your ethnic peculiarities when we get you back to our home base,' Penelope said unsympathetically.

'Do you think it'll sweep the planet?' Chris asked hopefully.

'I'm afraid you'll find we have more serious things on our minds than watching members of a primitive species demonstrating their barbarian heritage,' Penelope informed him, making it clear that she was one of those who took life seriously.

'But at the very least I should be besieged by hordes of worshipping females?' Chris suggested.

Penelope, with her weapon in her hand, obviously didn't feel any need to pull her punches. 'We have totally outgrown any interest in the male' she explained. 'It was all a matter of faulty glands.'

'She's telling you the truth there, I must agree,' Melmoth had to get his oar in.

Penelope showed no sign of gratitude for his support. 'Unfortunately your revolting planet adopted the wrong cure,' she pointed out.

Chris was understandably less than enthralled. 'You're not making it seem the most irresistible prospect,' he complained, 'I'm beginning to feel I'd rather stay with Paderewski here.'

Penelope, brandishing the laser-gun, said in her butch way 'You seem to forget who's in charge.'

'You seem to have forgotten that both our federations are signatories of a treaty by which we agree not to use force against members of a primitive species,' Melmoth pointed out quietly.

'Ah, but I happen to know what your real plans are for your young friend here,' Penelope said. She turned to Chris and looked significantly at him, so he in his turn looked at Melmoth and said 'Well, come on, give. What's this all about?'

Melmoth had the grace to look distinctly abashed, and remained silent.

After a short but meaningful pause, Penelope continued 'As he seems strangely unwilling to enlighten you, I suppose I'd better. You see, your friend over there decided it was too much bother sending you all the way back to his crummy home planet. He thought it'd be much less trouble to dispose of you here. Permanently. After he's had what he wants from you first, of course.'

Chris looked at Melmoth, who tried to explain 'I have to admit that was my original intention, until I got to know you rather better, and then ...'

But Chris cut him short, and turned to Penelope with 'Okay, you've made your point. Let's go.'

'There's just one little precaution we'd better take before we leave' she said, producing some cords, and handing one to Chris. 'If you would secure the good Captain here,' she suggested, which he did while she pointed the gun, then they did the same for Melmoth.

But before leaving she couldn't resist a little parting speech: 'Perhaps I may be excused for pointing out that if you hadn't let your animal lusts take precedence over your intellect, such as it is, you might well have been able to, ahem, dispose of him before I managed to get him safely on his journey. Instead he is joining us to help increase our strength against the day when we're ready to show you what we're made of.'

'Thank you, we don't want to know,' Melmoth retorted, but it was rather wasted on Penelope, who was already on her way out with Chris.

There were a few minutes of silence, with me keeping quiet to give Melmoth time to contemplate where his neglect of his duties had led. Then I remarked casually 'This isn't going to be considered one of your greatest successes.'

'Clever of you to notice,' Melmoth replied, but with less spirit than usual.

'They're going to be a bit worried back at G.H.Q. about Penelope's crowd getting hold of this one, aren't they, considering he showed such remarkably high potential?' I pressed on, doing my best to recall him to a sense of propriety.

But Melmoth was only concerned with was his own petty little personal affairs. 'I'm more worried that he's gone off without my having had the chance to tell him I'd given up all intention of cancelling him,' he told me.

'It's a trifle late to be recalled to a sense of duty,' I pointed out with justifiable acerbity.

But Melmoth, proving even more brazen than I could have imagined, explained 'O, don't be ridiculous. I wasn't proposing to send him back.'

'Then what exactly did you have in mind, sir?' I asked sarcastically.

'I still hadn't really worked out what I was going to do' Melmoth was confessing when Chris burst in and began untying him frantically, explaining as he did so 'I managed to give her the slip, via the back exit in the men's loo, but I don't suppose it will take her long to work out where I am.'

I was bewildered. 'What on earth have you come back for?' I asked, and Chris explained with primitive logic 'I couldn't leave him with his musical education only just begun.'

He had freed Melmoth, and was beginning to untie me when Melmoth stopped him, saying 'I think you'd better leave the good Captain as he is.'

'Why's that?' Chris asked before I did, and Melmoth explained 'He's not going to be too happy that we're going to run off with his only spacecraft.'

'You mean I'm really going to get a ride in a flying saucer?' Chris asked excitedly.

'We don't seem to have much option,' Melmoth replied.

'Where to?' Chris naturally wanted to know, but Melmoth had to admit that he hadn't had time to sort that out yet.

'Oh well, my horoscope said I was going to travel,' Chris said philosophically. 'Hey, though, wait a minute, what about your piano?'

Melmoth, who obviously has no sense of either decency or proportion, was insulted at this. 'I may not be the world's most efficient espionage chief,' he said reprovingly, 'but I do attend to all the really important details. There's one already on board: I used it to ease the monotony on the trip here.'

'Then lead on, Macduff,' Chris said enthusiastically. 'There's only one thing missing,' he added.

'What's that?' Melmoth asked.

'Your erstwhile assistant should be saying 'You won't get away with this,' Chris said, showing as little sense of the seriousness of what they were about to do as Melmoth himself.

'He knows we probably will,' Melmoth said optimistically. Then he turned to me and said 'Sorry about this, Captain, but I'm sure Penelope will release you if you speak nicely to her.'

'You'll be caught eventually,' I said, and they were gone.

It can't have been all that much later that Penelope burst in, though it felt quite a long time.

'Is he here? Has he been here? Where's Melmoth?' she practically screamed at me.

'I'll be more than happy to enlighten you while you're untying me,' I said with quiet dignity. She hesitated for a moment, then said grudgingly 'I suppose I may as well.'

While she was releasing me, I explained to her 'Melmoth says he's going to try and do a disappearing act with Chris. In our spaceship. If we hurry, we might be able to stop them.'

Now the initiative had been taken from her, she was much less decisive. 'But what do we do if we catch them?' she worried.

'Well, I certainly don't consider myself under Melmoth's orders, now he's deserted his post, so you can have him, and I'll deal with Chris,' I suggested.

But Penelope wasn't having any. 'No, no: it would be better if you took Melmoth back, so that he can be suitably punished for dereliction of duty,' she countered. 'Surely military protocol and all that is more important than one miserable Earthling?'

'I'm not letting you have Chris,' I said firmly, because if I could recapture him, I would obviously redeem myself with GHQ.

Penelope wasn't going to agree, and even threatened to tie me up again, but I'd taken the precaution of arming myself as soon as she'd freed me. 'Too late, I'm afraid,' I said.

'But we must come to some agreement before we catch them' she protested, and I pointed out that if we didn't reach one pretty soon, we weren't going to catch them at all.

'Well, be reasonable,' Penelope said plaintively: 'what earthly good is Melmoth to me?'

'You could have hours of innocent fun pointing out to each other the defects of your respective cultures,' I said teasingly.

I'm afraid we went on in this vein quite a while longer, by which time, of course, Melmoth and his wretched Earthling were well beyond our reach. But at least we eventually agreed on a less discreditable story to send back to our respective Headquarters. And, to look on the bright side, whoever they send as a replacement for Melmoth has got to be an improvement.

COMING OUT

'I can't understand where we went wrong,' George complained.

'You mustn't blame yourself,' his other half soothed.

'I'm wondering how long it's been going on behind our backs,' George continued. 'I just hope he's not been getting up to things here while we were out; that would be the last straw.'

'We've always encouraged him to feel that his bedroom was his own private place,' Jo said, seeking to mitigate the heinousness of the offence.

'There are limits to how much freedom one can grant.' George was making his position clear. 'After all, if we found out he was using it to make bombs for some terrorist group, we'd feel morally obliged to put a stop to it, wouldn't we?'

'That is a pretty extreme analogy,' Jo protested.

'I don't see that,' George argued. 'After all, it's a sort of moral bomb he's just detonated.'

'I thought we'd agreed that he was to be encouraged to make his own decisions?'

'Yes, but up till now he's always made the right ones. I never thought he would end up like this, or I wouldn't have agreed to it.'

'Now you're trying to have your cake and eat it.'

But George was not to be pacified. 'What he does when he's out is his own business, but I draw the line at having them both here. That would be condoning it. I don't think he realises how much this thing has upset me.

I don't know why he couldn't keep it quiet until he got his own place: then they could have set up together quietly without anything having actually come out into the open. He could still have come round here on his own: I wouldn't have gone round to his place, of course, not while they were living together, anyway, but at least it could all have been handled discreetly, instead of him being absolutely blatant about it.'

'You must give him some credit for having the courage to come out and tell us.'

'I think I'd rather he hadn't. If he's going to be that upfront about it, everybody's bound to know pretty soon. I can just imagine what it'll be like at my local. They won't say anything, probably, but they'll all be thinking we didn't make a proper job of bringing him up. I know what'll happen: there'll be a sudden hush when I enter, making it obvious what they've just been discussing. I shan't be able to enjoy going there any more. Children are so selfish: I don't suppose he's bothered to think for a moment what this is going to do to my social life.'

'It'll just be a nine-days wonder,' Jo soothed. 'Then they'll be onto something else.'

'Yes, but at the back of their minds they'll always be wondering where he got it from,' George complained, 'and probably imagining that I must have a taint of it somewhere. Me, who never even dabbled when I was a youngster, unlike quite a few I could name.'

Jo, choosing to assume this last was aimed generally rather specifically, tried to soothe him, suggesting 'Don't you think you're taking this too seriously? After all, I'm sure you're not exactly the first person this has happened to.'

'That is no consolation,' George responded.

'It could be just a phase,' Jo suggested pacifically. 'After all, he knows how strong your views are about that sort of thing, so he might be doing it just out of bravado, to assert his independence. I've noticed in other cases that, when someone has your sort of very definite opinions, and is always ready to thrust them down other people's throats, one is likely to provoke opposition. If I were you, I'd be inclined to bite my tongue, and let him get on with it. Then, most likely, in a few months he'll have got over it and be back to normal.'

'Yes, but supposing he doesn't?' George moaned. 'Then I'd be stuck with having to put up with it.'

'Which is more important, for him to do what you want him to do, or for him to be happy?' Jo asked

'For him to do what I want him to, of course,' George responded immediately. 'I cannot believe that a son of mine could seriously end up like — like that. It's not on the cards. I shall think seriously about disinheriting him if he persists: I didn't work as hard as I have to see my money go to that sort of set-up.'

'I had a word with his best mate John,' Jo told him. 'He's almost as unhappy about it as we are, but he hasn't struck him off his visiting list because of it, and in a way he's in a more vulnerable position than you, as far as what people are going to think.'

'He's not going the same way?' George enquired, obviously horror-struck at the possibility.

'There was no suggestion of that at all,' Jo assured him. 'In fact he seemed almost as upset as you.

'So presumably he's not the one who's led our boy astray.' George mused aloud. 'Who does that leave?'

'He couldn't have decided he was that way for himself?' Jo asked sceptically.

'If only he'd come to us at the beginning, when he first got some idea he might have that sort of tendency?' George ignored the suggestion. 'We might have been able to help him overcome it, send him to a Counsellor, perhaps even a sympathetic psychiatrist — I wouldn't have minded putting my hand in my pocket. I mean, it's not natural, in spite of what they say. They have to be led into it somehow. And it's not even as if he's been thrown into that sort of company: we don't mix in that kind of circle.'

'That's just from choice,' Jo expostulated, 'not a matter of moral principle. I'm sure some of them are perfectly pleasant.'

'That doesn't alter the fact that I feel he's let us down,' George was obviously going to get his moneysworth of feeling aggrieved. 'We've spent a small fortune on his upbringing, and this is how he rewards us.'

'That's the risk you take when you decide to have children,' Jo explained patiently. 'I seem to remember you were the one who thought it would be a good idea.'

'Not at all,' George protested energetically. 'I remember distinctly that you talked me into it.'

But Jo was not going to let him get away with that. 'On the contrary,' he was told 'I remember very clearly warning you that it would mean our having to deny ourselves a certain number of luxuries, and you said you were quite prepared for that.'

'Luckily my salary increases took care of that particular problem pretty quickly,' George commented smugly. 'But I did hope that at the least he would turn out to be a credit to us: really I think that's the least we were entitled to expect. And up till now I had high hopes.'

'Everyone has to be allowed one little weakness,' Jo suggested without too much conviction.

'Little weakness, perhaps,' George agreed. His voice took on a more sonorous note. 'Unfortunately that hardly seems the right term to describe this particular aberration. Not only that, he's compromised us as a family.'

'Children aren't computer programs, you know,' Jo argued. 'You may be able to influence them, but you can't completely control how they're going to turn out.'

'That's as may be,' George replied. 'All I can say is, I'd never have taken on the burden of fatherhood if I'd had the slightest intimation he was going to end up straight.'

COMMITMENT

From being an occasional indulgence, a casual popping-in to any cottage he happened to pass when he was in the area, it had gradually got to the status of a full-blown obsession. He knew it was out of control, but it didn't seem there was anything he could do about it. Several hours of each day were spent in this not particularly salubrious environment, with occasional interludes, none of them particularly protracted, at his place or some other guy's.

It was not as if he often got good or even reasonably good sex out of it, but that made no difference, and he came to realise that what turned him on was the scoring, adding another notch to his already outrageous chain of scalps. There had been some excuse at first. His last boy-friend had been one of those who was active mainly because he didn't like the idea of being passive, and would fuck because that was what gay men did. He didn't have a particularly interesting dick, and that, coupled with an even less interesting style of fucking, meant that it had been a purely rote performance for both of them, and hadn't happened at all frequently, mainly when Ralph thought he ought to be giving Dan his oats.

Dan had never bothered to explain to him that there were other ways gay men could satisfy each other, since Ralph's blowing technique was no better than his fucking, and Dan himself could never work up any great enthusiasm for working on Ralph's cock. So, while so far as he knew Ralph was monogamous, which in practice meant that he didn't seem to want sex much more often than once a month, Dan had to sneak most of his at any opportunity which presented itself, mostly during his lunch-hour, and on the way home from work.

Their affair had always been a bit one-sided, with Ralph much more attached to Dan than the other way around. So when one evening a couple of policemen called at the door and did their best to break the news gently that Ralph had been struck down by a car and died in the ambulance, Dan was quite surprised to find how upset he was.

Only that morning, as he had watched Ralph munching his way through his toast and Marmite, while dutifully listening to the news – Dan would much have preferred to have music on – he had once again chafed at the restrictiveness of their life together. But now that the bonds had been so brutally shattered, he felt mostly guilt that he hadn't been nicer to Ralph, a feeling intensified when he had to perform a formal identification of the body, and saw the injuries the car had inflicted.

In fact, it took him a good couple of months to get over the shock. The cremation did little to mitigate his sense of loss: there seemed something faintly bogus about it, and as he listened to the piped organ music and heard the eulogy delivered by a robed chaplain who had only too obviously never known Ralph, he regretted that he hadn't insisted on a proper burial, which would, as he knew from his parents' funerals, have had a cathartic effect.

Their affair had gone on for nearly ten years, and though Dan knew by that time that he had never really been in love with Ralph, he had kept the relationship going, mostly because he knew Ralph would have fallen to pieces without him. He wasn't the type to buck what he saw as his responsibility, and living together for that length of time had inevitably created emotional bonds, even if of another sort.

He was now thirty-six, no longer young so far as the gay scene was concerned, and for a while he felt resentful that his best cruising years had been spent tied to someone who had kept him off the scene, without offering much of what he had missed in return. But he wasn't the type to be hag-ridden by his past, so he shook off such thoughts, soon starting to make up for lost time. In particular a cottage only ten minutes' drive from where he lived, which had a fully justified reputation for popularity with married men wanting a taste of forbidden pleasures before abandoning themselves to the calls of domesticity, became his favorite haunt.

On the whole, the trade there wasn't bad: by no stretch of the imagination could Dan be called good-looking, but he was perfectly presentable, while he had a certain aura of confidence about him which proved, at least in this environment, a sufficient substitute for looks, since practically all those who were officially straight were after a change from their normal routine, and so found his style attractive. They would turn over without needing to be persuaded: not only that, but they were a lot less uninhibited about demonstrating that they were getting what they wanted. There was none of the reluctance to fully abandon themselves to their animal side that he had found in so many of his gay partners. He got better screwing in the next six months than he had ever had before.

Of necessity these were fleeting encounters, with no exchange of phone numbers: at the most they would part with an expressed wish to get together again on the part of one or both of them, but on Dan's side, at least, this wasn't very serious. Repeats never seemed to produce as good an experience as the first session, so he never sought them, and it was only rarely that he allowed himself to be trapped into one.

By this stage in his life he had got beyond the adolescent notion that he could only go with his 'type,' and he had tried out a wide variety of men. Two of his particular turn-ons were a masculine aura and a working-class background, but on the fortunately infrequent occasions when the available trade didn't qualify in either of these respects, he would usually allow himself to be satisfied with less essential characteristics. What he disliked most of all was any taint of effeminacy, but even that he could cope with if the alternative was nothing at all.

His social life took a back seat to this compulsion, and though he felt vaguely guilty about neglecting his friends, especially as he wasn't too keen to explain to them exactly what it was that he preferred to their company, it wasn't enough to get him to change. He got to recognise most of the men who used the place, and 'seconds' became a more frequent occurrence, out of necessity rather than choice. The excitement had long ago worn off, but he continued to haunt the place, with only occasional trips to other similar facilities.

Part of the reason for this preference was the fact that it lay further outside town than his home, so it was comparatively easy for him to drive there so long as he avoided the rush-hours, and he could park the car reasonably near, though not so near, he hoped and believed, that it was too obvious to the local residents what he was up to. Then, as he regularly assured himself, 'there weren't so many middle-class queens going there,' and there was some substance to this: even those who did appear from time to time, attracted no doubt by the same fetish that Dan demonstrated, were so obviously out of place that, even if they chanced to score, they rarely returned.

Dan of course didn't class himself with them, even though his parents would have been horrified to think he was putting so much effort into trying to be mistaken for a blue-collar worker, after they had made sure he got what they considered a good education. Certainly his habitual get-up of jeans and sneakers — the only time he donned a tie was for funerals — was practically the uniform for this particular occupation.

He was so used to this life-style that, when he first encountered Trevor, he looked on him only as a desirable piece of rough trade. This was not quite as surprising as it might seem, since Trevor, thorough in everything that he undertook, had dressed down for the occasion, arriving at the cottage in a pair of jeans with almost more holes than material, unshaven, and wearing a shirt that looked as if it was at least one trip to the laundry behind. But since these were accompanied by an arse to die for, as well as a reasonably impressive dick, he could have had any of the half-dozen guys currently on display even if his facial features had resembled King Kong's, though in fact he was more than presentable, with thick dark hair and full lips which were set off by a pair of particularly bright and expressive eyes.

Another attractive trait, at least so far as Dan was concerned, was that, unlike cottage queens in general, he didn't hang around on the very unlikely chance that his ideal would turn up. It took him no more than a couple of minutes to decide Dan was the one he wanted to go with, and only a very short while after that he was following Dan's Escort in his own rather ancient and battered Cortina.

The sex was not particularly wonderful: once they were in bed together, Trevor seemed somewhat different to the image he had putting over, but Dan was too used to that sort of disappointment to be particularly upset. When it was over, and they were dressing, he asked, more as ritual politeness than because he expected his offer to be taken up, 'Would you like a coffee, or did you want to get off?' and was quite surprised when his offer was accepted.

Trevor stayed for a good hour before he finally rose, saying with apparent reluctance 'I guess I have to be getting back, but I hope we'll meet again.' He followed this up by scribbling down his phone number, and passing it over to Dan, who found himself breaking with custom and replying in kind, though when Trevor had gone, he was still slightly puzzled as to why he'd done it.

He didn't, however, break with custom so far as to ring the number he'd been given, and he certainly hadn't expected Trevor to phone him a few days later and ask 'Do you fancy coming out for a drink?' Even stranger was the fact that just the suggestion gave him an instant hard-on, especially considering their sexual styles hadn't really gelled. He couldn't remember the last time that he had got excited over a specific prospect rather than just general cruising, but he managed to take up the offer without displaying too much eagerness — coolness was all in his world of one-night-stands — and a few nights later they were again in bed together.

This time things went much better; Trevor was more sure of himself, and Dan guessed that he was one of those who functioned better when he'd got to know someone. He was flattered and impressed that Trevor had already got a fair idea of Dan's sexual tastes, and when it became obvious that he was planning to stay the night, Dan decided, after an initial feeling of being trapped, that he rather liked the idea.

He had expected just one more round, but in fact, they were good for several: the sex got better each time, and Trevor proved such an enthusiastic lover that Dan was almost over-faced. After so many years of perfunctory sex, he had almost forgotten what a totally different experience it could be when both participants were fully involved. By the time their physical charge had been diminished by a couple of orgasms each, they were able to move onto some of the finer points of love-making, paying more than cursory attention to each other's needs and preferences, so that by the time of their last bout, in the early morning, they had inevitably grown a lot closer to each other.

All that day at work, Dan's mind kept reverting to Trevor, and he started turning over in his mind the pros and cons of having a relationship, even though he kept reminding himself it was far too early to be thinking about anything of the sort. Nothing was settled; Trevor might just be after a fling, and not want to settle down. But that didn't alter the fact that he had begun to fancy the idea, and if the chance came, he wasn't going to turn it down.

He had already realised that rough trade wasn't really an appropriate classification for Trevor: in fact, Trevor's mother would have been just as horrified as Dan's to hear him described in such terms. She had come from a nice middle-class family, and married beneath her, an attractive, masculine, good-natured man, but of the artisan class.

She had never regretted it: so far as she could tell her marriage was a good deal more successful than that of most of her friends, but she was still very conscious of the gap. So she had done her best to see that their only child should not be disadvantaged by it, and he had received a proper middle-class education, in due course getting a proper middle-class job.

Trevor, though, preferred his father's side of the family, and when with them was able to talk and act like them, even behave as if he thought like them. His mother couldn't imagine for a moment why he should want to, and he didn't bother to explain to her that it was, incidentally, a considerable asset on the gay scene. Certainly it had attracted Dan's attention, and by the time he realised the truth Dan was already hooked.

They had only spent a few more nights together, with each time their coupling growing more exciting and involving, before Trevor confronted Dan to ask him point-blank if he was serious.

'I can't go on like this,' he announced bluntly. 'You'll have to make up your mind whether we're to be an item, or else I'm going to have to stop seeing you, cos I'm getting too damn involved.'

Dan was about to reply in the affirmative as lightly as he could, professions of love and involvement having always been difficult for him, when Trevor put up a hand to stop him.

'Before you say anything, I'd better tell you that I'm monogamous in an affair, and I would expect the same from my other half. I rather think you're something of a cottage queen: I've nothing against it, but I couldn't have a lover who was doing that while he was with me.'

The glamour had rather gone off cottaging for Dan since he had met Trevor; it now seemed distinctly pointless and cheap, so he was quite happy to agree and promise to give it up. After that, all proceeded pretty smoothly, and eventually, when they had been together for nearly six months, Trevor, who had been living with his parents again, after the breakup of his last relationship, moved in with Dan, and they settled down to the life of a married couple.

During their first year together, all went well. Dan was surprised how easily he slipped back into being a married man. Of course there were occasional moments, usually after they had some sort of tiff, and he was feeling temporarily pissed off with Trevor, when he regretted the loss of his freedom, and fancied a quick trip to the cottage. For quite a while he managed to keep this impulse in check, but one day, after a minor argument over nothing much at all, mainly because Trevor had had a bad day at work and was inclined to take it out on Dan, he took advantage of Trevor's attendance at his Keep-fit class, which he was religious about, to pay a visit to his old haunt, and see how it was ticking over.

The trade on offer was not interesting, and when he compared it with his lover, the contrast was so ridiculous that he came away without doing anything, and was watching the tele, with a clear conscience, when Trevor returned home in contrite mood. They ended up making slow affectionate love which, Dan knew very well, was infinitely better than anything he could have snatched at the cottage.

None the less, the dam had been breached, and over the next few months he made a number of surreptitious visits there, though he didn't always end up having sex. Every time he did, he would regret it afterwards, for it would always leave him feeling cheap and defiled. But inevitably it meant that he would only rarely initiate love-making with Trevor, and quite often not respond to his overtures either. The crunch came when, one evening, he returned from one of these forays to find Trevor sitting there looking very black indeed, and with a business-like leather strap on his knee: he had felt impelled to cut his class to check up on Dan, and all his worst fears were now confirmed.

'You've been cottaging,' he stated baldly, and Dan hadn't the face to deny it.

'I knew you'd been getting up to things,' Trevor told him. 'You were crazy to think you could hide it from me. If this means you want me to move out, I'll go tomorrow.'

'Of course it doesn't,' Dan cried. 'I love you.'

He hadn't realised, until he said it, that it was true enough for the thought of losing him to be genuinely horrifying.

'But not enough to keep away from the cottage, it seems,' Trevor said unbendingly.

All Dan could say was 'I'm sorry. I know I shouldn't have done it.'

'I told you I couldn't handle it,' Trevor said. 'But I love you, so I'll give you a choice. Either you solemnly promise me never to do it again, and I give you a damn good thrashing, or we call it a day and I move out tomorrow.'

'You're not serious,' Dan blustered. 'It didn't mean anything, and you know it didn't.'

'It meant something to me, and you knew it did,' Trevor reminded him.

'I'll promise not to go there again,' Dan offered. 'You don't need to use that thing on me.'

Trevor shook his head. 'It's the whole package or nothing,' he said

Dan lifted the strap off Trevor's knee, and ran his fingers over it. It was about eighteen inches long and four inches wide while, though the leather was fairly soft, it was also quite thick. He imagined it landing on his arse, and flinched at the thought. He had at least two acquaintances who would have been in the seventh heaven to be involved in this present scenario, but any kind of pain was a complete turn-off for him; he didn't even like having his nipples tweaked, or a spot of light biting, during love-making.

'How many?' he asked, still holding the strap.

But Trevor shook his head.

'You'll have to find that out,' he said.

'I'm not letting you use that thing on me,' Dan protested. 'I'm not a fucking schoolboy.'

Trevor remained silent, waiting for Dan's decision.

Dan said nothing for a long time, trying to make up his mind. Eventually he said 'How do I know you won't go absolutely over the top?'

'You don't,' Trevor agreed.

'Tell you what, I'll take six and we'll call it quits.'

Trevor didn't answer.

'Alright, then, a dozen, but that's my limit' he offered desperately, cringing mentally even as he suggested it.

When there was still no response he burst out hysterically 'What more do you want? You know I don't want to lose you, but you're being unreasonable.'

'You have to trust me and leave it up to me what I do,' Trevor said.

'I do in everything else,' Dan protested. 'You know I do. But you're so angry I'm frightened of what you might do.'

'Whose fault is that?' Trevor demanded.

'I know, I know,' Dan agreed. 'That doesn't stop me being scared.'

But Trevor was implacable, and after some moments of agonised hesitation Dan knew he had no option; whatever it cost he mustn't lose Trevor, so he asked submissively 'What do you want me to do?'

'Strip off and lie down on the bed,' Trevor told him.

They both made their way into the bedroom, where Trevor produced some short lengths of rope while Dan was getting his clothes off. That added another notch to his frightened anticipation, but in a way he was also relieved, because it meant he wouldn't be able to disgrace himself by not being able to take what Trevor was going to hand out. So he obediently lay face down, when Trevor fixed his arms and legs to the corners of the bed.

But by that time Trevor had got what he wanted, the reassurance that he was still Dan's number one priority, and that Dan had realised it. The rest was only window-dressing; nevertheless he gave Dan a couple of strokes with the strap, hard enough to bring home to him the reality of the situation. But they were nothing like as hefty as they could have been, and then he threw the strap down, kissed him, and released him from the ropes, to join him on the bed.

COMPUTER CHOICE

It was an unexpected stroke of luck that the new Disney film opened at their local cinema just in time, on the last day of the fair. His detestation of Uncle Walt's products was sufficiently well established for him to be able to refuse convincingly to accompany the rest of his family, though he made sure to give them extra for popcorn or whatever, so that they wouldn't feel they were losing out. Then, as soon as he had dropped them off, he drove quickly to where the fair was temporarily situated

He walked round practically the whole of the perimeter, past all sorts of attractions which he only afforded sufficient attention to confirm that they weren't what he had been told to look for, till at last he found it, between 'Mysto, Palm-reader and Clairvoyant,' and 'The Living Fossil.' The board outside the tent displayed the legend 'Gypsy Lavengro can change your life' but it did nothing to daunt him; he parted the flap and walked in.

Inside he was met by a Mediterranean-looking man, with a moustache and a full head of dark black hair, who asked him in a very flat voice, though with no trace of a foreign accent, 'Did you want a full reading, or just the short one?' Rob produced the coin he had been given all those months ago, and handed it over to the gypsy, who pocketed it and immediately took him behind a curtain, where a computer monitor and keyboard rested on a table, with cables at the back attached to nothing that Rob could recognise.

The putative gypsy picked up some sort of metal helmet, handing it to him with instructions to put it on his head. Meanwhile he plugged the cable extending from it into the side of the monitor, while Rob sat down at the table, and then began to tell him about the programme that he was about to run.

But Rob wasn't really listening: the menu on the screen seemed quite sufficiently clear for him to get going straightaway, and with a few clicks of the mouse it was up and running. The main screen disappeared, and he gave an involuntary gasp: there on the screen was his wife, and in the near distance he could see his two children playing. She was reading a magazine, with her hair in curlers. The picture was so lifelike that he knew it couldn't be computer-generated graphics: there had to be some form of direct linkage to his own imaging system. But he had no time to marvel at the sophistication of the technology, for suddenly he was part of the scene he was viewing. Then, as he stood there, his wife turned and called out to him 'Oh, there you are, dear: the lawn needs cutting today.'

'Very well, dear,' he agreed, going over to the garden shed. Magnolia, his daughter, came running up to tell him about the gymkhana she had entered for. He listened with one ear, while running over in his mind what Jenkins at the office had said about the possible move to Andover: it certainly looked as if it might do him a spot of good, if he could only persuade Rachel it was in all their interests.

In the event, Rachel proved amenable enough: it was Tom, who had just been made a junior monitor at school, and so was enjoying the pleasure of throwing his weight about, who objected most strongly, even though his parents took the trouble to explain just why the move was essential for them. Eventually Rob had to ignore him and his fits of temper, going ahead in spite of them.

The results bore out his choice: within the year he had received promotion, as well as a considerable salary increase, while greater responsibility merely made the job more interesting. Rachel, too was happier: whereas she had been nobody in particular in the metropolis, she blossomed in the more limited environment of a small town.

True, there seemed to be little time for his musical interests: his piano-playing worsened as he stopped practising, but the increased family harmony — apart from Tom, who was still sulking about the move — had to be worth it. Then one day, he went into his office as usual, but instead of the standard opening screen, he found himself staring at the menu he had first seen on the gypsy's computer. He looked around: he was back in the tent.

It took him some little while to re-adjust; the experience he had just gone through had seemed so real. But eventually he was able, with the aid of a certain amount of will-power, to turn his attention back to the menu, which now was showing a number of options offering to change what he had just experienced. He explored the possibilities through a number of sub-menus, and decided to try a first alteration: he expunged Tom, and went back to the main screen.

The sequence it led into, though, was a different one altogether: a night from early in their marriage, when he was still having regular sex with Rachel. Even while he enjoyed it, he found himself reflecting that there seemed to be a large element of the mechanical in the performance, and afterwards he suffered from what the Romans had characterised so well, a feeling of post coitum triste.

This scene ended, and he was staring at the main screen once more, wondering why the machine had selected that particular part of his life. He recalled enough, from the man's introductory spiel, to realise that they were areas of unresolved concern to him. He stared at the options menu until his eyes began to feel the strain, but chose none of them, merely clicked for another main sequence.

This time he was at the office, where he was discussing with a couple of his colleagues, in an atmosphere of utmost seriousness and dedication, the marketing strategy for the next addition to their range of convenience foods. Now that they had got all the mileage they could out of the 'no artificial additives' line, as had all their competitors, what was to be the next gimmick?

The scene came to a halt. Rob knew now what was happening: the damnable machine was indeed picking up on the sorest points of his existence, and the effect was to accentuate the feeling he sometimes got, when on his own, that the whole thing was a ridiculous charade. But what was the good of that? His choices had been made. Maybe with hindsight they had proved to be bad choices, but he was stuck with them, and he couldn't see it getting him anywhere to explore the area of 'if only.' He had acquired a wife and child, and that was it.

The so-called gypsy interrupted his musings. 'You have five minutes left,' he announced.

'I might as well use them,' Rob thought to himself, and with one bold stroke eradicated his marriage. After he had sent the command, though, he couldn't face being tantalised with how things might have turned out, and instead of activating the follow-on sequence to see what sort of difference it would make to his life, he just sat and gazed into space, thinking with some bitterness of how much of a con life really was.

A bell pinged, and the monitor reverted to its loading screen. The gypsy came round and helped Rob remove the headpiece. Then he gave him a card similar to the one he had inserted into the computer at the beginning, only this time it was red, and a coin like the one Rob himself had been given.

'The card is for your use if you wish to visit my tent when I am here again. The coin is for you to give to the person who most needs it,' the gypsy told him.

'How will I know him?' Rob asked, puzzled.

'You will know him,' the gypsy assured him.

Rob thanked him mechanically and went out of the tent, still in something of a brown study. But by the time he reached his comfortable bachelor flat, he had already decided that, after his next concert, he would have a nice long holiday somewhere very isolated, where he could really get the seclusion he enjoyed.

A FEW SNAPS

I don't think I was cut out by Nature to be a bachelor — actually I've taken to describing myself self-deprecatingly as a grass-widower, since at the moment I see Grace quite infrequently. In fact, I think Timmy, my son, sees more of her than I do, but we have plans to change that after we've let a few months go by. Grace assures me I have no reason to feel jealous, even though I confess to having been thrown a trifle off-balance by some of the items she has given him for his wardrobe, particularly those I happen to know he keeps hidden underneath his clean shirts.

Of course there is also Diana, and I enjoy my fatherly privileges like any normal father, but she is growing up fast, and already showing signs of being more interested in a boy-friend nearer her own age. She is a very self-assured young lady, thanks in no small measure, I believe, to her upbringing, and as a modern father I am particularly pleased that she has taken feminist thinking so thoroughly on board. Mildred had to go to Women's Self-Assertion classes for more than two years before she could pluck up the courage to assault men when they failed to pay her the respect due to her as a woman.

The magic went out of our marriage some years ago, and since then we'd rather been in the doldrums, until Mildred found out that the parents of a new friend of hers, Rochelle, ran an escort agency from their council flat in Camberwell. She expressed curiosity about its workings, as one does and, to cut a long story short, they offered to place us on their books as a 'mature couple'.

I would not have considered the idea for a moment, had it not been that I had been made redundant some months earlier, and the miserable severance pay I had received did not look as if it was going to take us very far — Mildred always had rather expensive tastes. So we talked it over and agreed to try it, rather nervously at first.

Life has never been the same since. Though we are both in our forties and thus, I had assumed, over the hill as far as that sort of work was concerned, the reality turned out to be far from the case. Our clients were, as expected, mostly male, which was really more interesting for Mildred than me, though I found that an element of healthy competitiveness did wonders towards re-kindling interest in the proceedings. But sometimes it would be a couple, which I, of course, found a good deal more exciting, and initially I was quite taken aback to discover just how wild were the fantasies that some of them came along with.

When we first started, I had been pretty unsure how I would be able to cope with the demands of the work, but to my surprise and relief I found that the wilder the scenario, the surer the certainty that I would be up to it, and I think Mildred was pleasantly surprised, not to say impressed, with just what I showed myself capable of. To do her justice, she did not lag behind, and I think our clients, at any rate after the first two or three, when we were a spot tentative, all felt that they had got good value.

Mind you, some of the rougher activities did sometimes mean that I had to curtail my sunbathing sessions, or risk attracting unwanted attention, but I felt it was worth that little sacrifice. And the agency found its business expanding sufficiently that they took on Mildred's sister, Grace, as a dominatrix, when they heard from Mildred that she had displayed tendencies of that sort from an early age.

Grace took to the work like a duck to water, and before long had combined it with one of her hobbies, opening a page on the Internet called Execution, which title, I may remark, did not refer to computer programs. Indeed, I believe its main attraction to be the distinctly gory pictures she has loaded on from her collection, some of which make me feel quite queasy.

Then she soon got busy compiling a CD-Rom of the same sort of material, which she was certain would be a popular under-the-counter item in many backstreet bookshops, while her husband, Jack, as usual trying to jump on the latest bandwagon, came up with the idea of a sort of do-it-yourself executioner's kit which, he told us, he expected to be able to sell at the most outrageous profit margin. Frankly, even with the wider experience of life I have gained since working for the agency, I found it difficult to imagine what sort of person could possibly be interested in the rather extreme items he said he was working on.

I'm afraid I never really took to Jack, one of that strange band of men who, though noticeably effeminate, is still as interested in the fair sex as the rest of us. Unlike a normal man, though, Jack actually preferred the company of women to that of men. Mildred of course doted on him — a strange thing I've noticed is that women in general seem to prefer men with at least a touch of ponciness in their make-up — but I found his rather oleaginous charm totally resistible. Jack's only real talent had to be a line in convincing patter which had, on more than one occasion, operated to the financial detriment of members of his own family, which tells you what sort of man he was, and I suppose I ought really to have been on my guard with him this time. But he was, as usual, very persuasive and, as it was Jack's idea, my wife was immediately enthusiastic.

'All I need, old chap,' he explained with that air of bonhomie which seemed to open so many doors for him, 'is a few snaps to whet the appetite, and I know the orders will come pouring in. I mean, look at this.'

What he showed me was a not unskilfully executed sketch of a rather appalling-looking contraption, with the half-nude victim's body secured by an inordinate number of leather straps, and with various attachments all over the place. This, he informed me with pride, was what he had finally come up with, an All-Purpose Executioner's Kit which could do what he casually referred to as 'the job ' in getting on for a dozen different ways.

'If you think I'm letting myself get anywhere near that thing,' I exclaimed with fully justified apprehension, 'you're right out of your mind.' And I went on to suggest 'Why don't you ask Grace?' confident in the knowledge that she knew Jack far too well to indulge him in any of his schemes.

'She's already refused,' he explained, quite unabashed. 'But she suggested that, in your line of work, you would be quite likely to come across someone who'd be prepared to model for us. Perhaps you could offer them a free session or something?.'

Free sessions were not an idea I was prepared to consider for a moment, and anyway, as I pointed out to him, Grace's clients were the likeliest source of volunteers. My experience of the vivid imaginations possessed by some of our clients made me feel pretty certain that not only would she be able to find a candidate willing to pose in situ, she might even find someone who would be willing to pay handsomely for the privilege.

In the event, getting hold of a suitable candidate proved even easier than I had anticipated. In no time at all, we were in receipt of a mini-deluge of offers, and we arranged meetings with a couple of the most promising. The first one seemed to me to be too melodramatic in his approach, and I had a feeling he might let us down at the last minute, but the other one, a good deal older, so hopefully with a more mature attitude, did seem quite as sane as I felt we could reasonably expect. He also proved to have suitable premises, where we could erect Jack's contraption and take the pictures.

I was surprised to find that Jack actually had produced quite a practical working-model — either that or he'd conned someone into doing it for him. It was all in pieces when we went round to collect it — in my car, of course — but when we got to our rendezvous, and took it down into this Simon's large and suitably atmospheric cellar, it proved reasonably easy to assemble, on top of which it looked quite capable of doing the business.

I was slightly appalled to find that it would in fact genuinely perform all the functions it advertised, but Jack explained to me that the customers he had in mind wouldn't be fobbed off with mere imitations; they would expect the real thing. He also confided that he was going to try and sell it to terrorist groups as part of their field kit. What little I knew about such organisations made me think that they were more than fully supplied in this area, but I didn't feel this was the right moment to pour cold water on Jack's enthusiasm.

Our punter, when we discussed the arrangements beforehand, seemed surprisingly matter-of-fact, and if I hadn't known what strange fantasies he harboured, I would certainly never have guessed. Grace had declined to be present at the photo-shoot, but she lent Mildred a number of items that she used with her clients. So while I strapped Simon in the chair, and fixed up the first device on the menu, which Jack had decided should be the garrotte, Mildred changed into a little black lingerie number, topped off by a black leather mask which, though not covering much of her face, nonetheless did render her unrecognisable.

For these first pictures, Jack had provided Simon with an upper-head mask, finishing above the chin, so that the prospective purchaser could get a good view of the device in operation. And as soon as he was happy with his lighting and the camera angle, he gave Mildred the signal to go ahead, when she began turning the screw with what, I would have said, were somewhat inappropriately dainty movements. They seemed to do the job, though, because Simon began choking and gurgling in no time, but as we were not making a video, and so any sound-effects would be quite lost, all we needed was just a couple of shots showing the device in operation. However, Mildred, I noticed with a certain dismay, was unable to resist giving the screw one more little turn after Jack had said to stop, and I thought to myself I would make sure never to let her talk me into any pursuits of the sort.

Next he decided we should work on the guillotine, but Simon, after experiencing Mildred's excess of enthusiasm, didn't seem inclined to trust her any further, and it took quite a time to persuade him to go on with the shooting. Eventually he agreed, but then once again I had to do all the work of strapping him in place, while she touched up her makeup and primped her hair. I tested the edge of the blade with my thumb after I'd finished, and it didn't seem to me to be particularly sharp, which I would have thought would mean that it was likely to get buried in the victim's neck rather than slicing it right off, but then it would be just like Jack to economise on that sort of detail.

For this one Simon was dressed up in a full head mask, with gaps for the eyes, nose, and mouth. Jack had managed to borrow, from somewhere, one of those high-speed cameras that are used for sports photography so, after he'd taken one picture of Mildred standing looking down at her victim, he gave her the signal to release the catch, and the blade came whizzing down at a rate of knots, to be stopped, at the last moment, by the safety-catch just half-an-inch or so above Simon's neck.

But the excitement was evidently too much for him, since he gave a great gasping moan and passed out. I hurriedly untied him, got the mask off, and looked anxiously to see whether he'd been so disobliging as to die on us, but, thank heavens, he was still breathing. We unstrapped him, and lifted his limp form into an easy chair.

It was really rather awkward, since even Jack didn't dare take the risk of him actually croaking if we tried him in another scene. Instead he suggested, in as encouraging a manner as he could manage, since I imagine he knew beforehand what my answer would be, that I might like to take Simon's place, but I refused point-blank. With a slight inner smile, I pointed out to him that I was perfectly competent with a camera, if he wished to continue the session.

Jack being the sort of person who always tries to ensure that someone else is sitting in the hot seat, I quite enjoyed watching him squirm at my logical suggestion. He even tried to get Mildred to do it, but for once she was able to resist his blandishments, and so eventually, with many admonitions to us as to how extremely careful we must be, he allowed us to strap him into position for the third set of pictures.

The lethal injection module was considered to be insufficiently exciting from the purely visual angle, so we next moved onto the rather grandly-titled Portable Gas Chamber. Obviously a real one was out of the question, so what he had devised was a large transparent plastic bag which fitted over the victim's head and could be tied securely at the neck. The ingenious part was a self-sealing valve through which a suitably poisonous gas could be squirted. But no sooner had we got the bag on his head than he started to make a fuss, yelling out something about suffocating, I think, though in fact there was quite enough air inside the bag to last him while we took the snaps, so long as he didn't get too over-excited.

Because he was over-reacting in this really rather ridiculous way, I couldn't resist a little joke: I squirted a spot of after-shave that I had bought that day through the valve. Really I've never seen such an exhibition of panic: anyone would have thought it was prussic acid from the fuss he made, though how he imagined I could be carrying that sort of thing about with me I can't imagine. The temptation was intense, on my part at least, to let him savour the experience, but Mildred, who has never displayed much of a sense of humour, didn't seem to find it particularly amusing, and removed the bag before I'd even taken the snaps.

I tried pointing out to Jack that the sort of expressions he had just displayed were exactly what we wanted for advertising purposes, but he flatly refused to have the bag on again, and though I tried to persuade him, it was a lost cause, especially as Mildred, true to type, supported him. So I just suggested we move on to the next module, the Electric Chair.

Jack was quite jittery by this time, and even tried to stop me putting the plug in the socket. But this meant the red warning light wouldn't come on, greatly reducing the effectiveness of the tableau, and eventually he was forced to see reason and let me switch on, an action made easier by the fact that he was strapped in securely, and so hardly in a position to stop me.

To give him his due, the pictures I got of him there were really convincing: he gave every impression of being absolutely terrified. As we were using a digital camers, we were able to look at the results immediately, and I must say it's a thousand pities that so far we haven't been able to use them.

Really, I still don't quite know how it happened, but when I was getting Mildred to pose beside Jack, with her finger resting just above the switch, I somehow lost my balance, and fell in such a way that I landed with my weight pressing down on her finger, so that the current came on, and Jack immediately started twitching, while a split second later Mildred fell against him, going into spasms in her turn.

I know Grace is quite convinced that I did it deliberately, but in fact I was only just able to disengage myself in time, while the two of them were yelling out to me to switch the current off before it was too late. But I knew that, if I did, they were both going to be awfully cross, perhaps even attempt violence on my person, when I would be in an extremely vulnerable position with the two of them to my one, so I just went back to the camera and took some more shots, because I felt certain that sooner or later, when it seemed safe enough, I would be able to dispose of the whole collection for a nice little sum. I kept going as long as I could, but eventually the smell of burning flesh became quite unpleasant, so I left the room and went to the kitchen.

I noticed, as I was going out, that Simon had recovered consciousness and was half-sitting up, staring in fascination at the result of my little mishap, so when I made myself a pot of tea, I poured a cup out for him as well. The two bodies seemed quite inert by now, which meant it was safe for me to go over and switch the current off. The smell, a distinctly distasteful one, was even stronger by that time, so I helped Simon to the kitchen, where I sat him in a chair, and started discussing how we should handle the consequences of our unfortunate accident.

I can't say he was at all co-operative at first, but eventually, after I had pointed out to him that it had all happened on his premises, and that no one would ever believe he had been a non-participant, he agreed to my digging up some of the cellar floor and burying them there. Luckily it is quite cool, so that the bodies wouldn't decompose too quickly, and I didn't have to go mad and attend to it all at once, especially as the digging and so on, for which Simon wasn't really in any condition to assist me, was hot work. Once I had finished the re-cementing, though, a couple of days later, no one would really have known anything of the sort had ever happened there.

But I'm rushing on ahead. When I'd done some initial cleaning up and left Simon's place, I went round and told Grace that the dream that we had for so long thought impossible of achievement had suddenly started to come wonderfully true. And in fact, as I said, she thinks I did it on purpose, and really I believe she rather admires me for it. As she had only married Jack on the rebound from losing me to Mildred, she wasn't too shattered. We decided to let it be known that the two of them had run off together, and as we both knew they had been conducting a clandestine affair under our noses, in the complacent belief that we knew nothing about it, and of course a number of the neighbours had been well aware of this fact even before we were, we thought it would sound plausible enough, and so it has proved.

Grace ransacked Mildred's wardrobe to make it look as if she had taken a lot of her clothes, and I did the stricken husband bit. Even though it would have made sense financially, we have decided not to live together in case some evil-minded old biddy should get suspicious. One or two people have apparently been round looking for Jack, but we think that was because he owed them money, and apart from that, it all seems to have gone down very well. Probably what will eventually happen is that Grace will move in with me, so that the children will have someone to mother them, but she will have her own room, and we won't get married, as we don't want to set tongues wagging.

However, yesterday I read in my newspaper that an elderly man had been found suffocated in his cellar. According to the report, foul play was not suspected, and the area mentioned was Finsbury Park, where Simon lived, so I think, and Grace agrees with me, that he must have been living out one of his fantasies again.

I drove past there this morning to cast an eye, and saw a For Sale board up. My initial reaction was one of panic, though a few moments' reflection sufficed to reassure me that the likelihood of the new owners digging up the cellar is pretty remote. I mean, there's no reason why they should, and we'd have to be very unlucky for it to happen. But, just to be on the safe side, I popped into a travel agent on my way back and got some info about flights to South America. I shan't mention that to Grace, though: at this stage I prefer to keep all my options open.

FROM THE DIARY OF AN ARTIST

So there I was in the artist's room, and the only telegrams waiting for me were one from my agent and one I'd had the forethought to organise myself. In a brief moment of weakness, I found myself almost regretting getting rid of Roger: at least he used to send goodwill messages on these occasions. But when he began resenting the fact that my career was taking off, so that I was unable to accompany him to the various low haunts which constituted his extremely plebeian idea of entertainment, I had no option but to break it off.

At the same time, I couldn't help reflecting yet again on the self-centredness of other people. I don't allow myself to get bitter, but many's the time I've popped into my neighbour's for some butter or sugar or something, not to mention the times I've remembered to pay her back; yet, even though I had mentioned to her more than once in the past few weeks that I had this important recital coming up, she couldn't be bothered to send a card, let alone a telegram.

I suppose I should have expected no better, though. She would never ask me how I was getting on; I always had to offer the information. Obviously she's so obsessed by her own little difficulties that she hasn't any time or energy to spare for thinking about other people. Yet it was this monster in human form who had the gall to tell me I was totally wrapped up in myself, and not at all sympathetic when it came to the problems of others!

So that you should know just what an outrageous libel that was, I'll give you an example of the caring sort of person that I am. When my sister phoned to tell me that our Mother was on the way out — and let's face it, being well into her seventies, she could have done the decent thing years ago, not hung on out of sheer cussedness —- did I not jump into my old banger and pop down to see her, just as soon as I'd lined up a couple of other worthwhile visits in the area?

While I was at it, I also took the opportunity to organise a visit to a former piece of trade in my old haunts, which in the event proved to be not really worth the bother. I found he'd done nothing to improve his performance since the last time I visited him, even though on that occasion I had dropped a couple of hints about possible ways in which he could tighten up his act. Tactfully, of course; I don't like hurting people's feelings — not that he'd demonstrated much evidence of possessing any worth mentioning.

Anyway, as I was saying, as soon as all that had been organised, I zipped off down there. And when I arrived at her bijou Old People's Home, did I say what was in my mind, along the lines of 'Come on, you silly old bag, it's time you popped your coil.' No, of course I didn't: I even took her some fruit down in case she could eat it — mangoes, a particular favourite of mine, which was lucky, as she didn't seem to be in any condition to appreciate my thoughtful gesture.

Since she was still lucid — not that she'd ever displayed any great ability in that area — and a bit down, it seemed to me, I did my best to cheer her up, explaining that she could die happy, since she had fulfilled the purpose of her time on this earth by giving birth to me. Then I went on to tell her my really exciting news, that I was at last really beginning to achieve some sort of success, and how my recital on the twenty-eighth bode fair to be an important milestone in my career, while engagements were beginning to be offered with gratifying frequency. Not that my talent had come from her side of the family; still, you'd have thought this would be a real tonic to anyone imbued with the true ethos of motherhood.

But all she could go on about was her aches and pains, and what the doctor had said, and how the nurses weren't as sympathetic as they might be. So I attempted to lighten her mood by encouraging her to look on the bright side of it all, namely the fact that she wouldn't be called on to endure it for very much longer. However, she was obviously determined to be miserable, and wouldn't let any of my light-hearted banter cheer her up. I expect, though, that after I left, and she had time to reflect properly on what I had said, that it would help to give her the strength to go calmly to whatever awaited her — nothing spectacularly interesting, I've no doubt.

I've had to learn to be tough and self-reliant in this harsh world of ours, so I didn't let any of these domestic happenings dampen my spirits. When the time came, I went out there and gave my audience of my best. And I'm glad to say that they at least were appreciative: I played three encores, and some of them would have liked another but, not wanting to satiate them with delight, I thought it better to leave them still hankering.

After such a triumph, I didn't fancy just going home to my solitary pad, so I popped along to one of my regular haunts, picked up some member of what are laughably called the labouring classes, took him home, and screwed him silly, with probably a greater expenditure of calories on my part than he would use up during his whole working week. Unfortunately I was so exhausted by all this, on top of everything else, that I hadn't the energy to get rid of him in the usual way, which meant that I had the unpleasant experience of waking up the next morning to find his head on the pillow next to mine, and thus being forced to a salutary realisation of what one's glands will do to lower one's standards.

I toyed with the thought of revealing to him who I am, after which he would go no doubt home to write in his diary — assuming he was sufficiently literate to keep one — that he'd been screwed by a great artist on the threshold of a triumphant career. But he probably couldn't have spelt half the words, and anyway who'd bother to read his inelegant maunderings? I made a cup of tea, as well as some effort to respond to his chatter, which was quite a struggle, as it concerned matters of no conceivable interest whatever. Eventually I managed to despatch him to surroundings no doubt more suitable for one of his non-intellectual cast.

He gave me his phone number when he departed, and obviously hoped to receive mine. I hadn't the heart to disappoint him, so I gave him my next door neighbour's, thinking that she'd probably be glad of the chance to have a little chat with someone. I mean, he was quite sweet, but as far as I was concerned, his life had had its glorious moment: to attempt to repeat it would be to give him notions above his proper station in life.

Then, when he'd finally gone, I nipped next door just to let her know how successful my concert had been. She did her best not to look impressed, but I'm quite sure she was, and anyway I felt it my duty as a good neighbour to keep her in touch.

Yet when I gave her the bottle of extra-strength aspirins I'd thoughtfully remembered to buy for her, since she was always complaining about being in pain, she thanked me in the most cursory manner imaginable. All she seemed to want to talk about was what they had said to her at the Hospital, but as she hadn't even bothered to get out of bed to make me a welcoming cup of coffee, I cut her short on this. Anyway, it was only encouraging her to be morbid, so I pointed out, in the nicest kind of way, how insignificant her own little problems would appear if she could only manage to look at from the perspective of the whole grand scheme of things. Then I encouraged her to look on the bright side, and returned home to make my own drink.

To be frank, I'm not entirely sure what the bright side of terminal cancer is, but trying to find it is bound to take her mind off her aches and pains for a while, thus doing her some good. Anyway, I couldn't afford any more time for social chitchat: I had to start preparing my next programme.

THE GIFT

It was a nice funeral. Everyone was happy, as happy as Arnold had been confident they would be, otherwise he would never have done what he had done, but it was still good to have it confirmed.

He scanned through the assembly of mourners. Sarah Wilkins, the dead woman's daughter, was tearful and weepy, but underneath Arnold could tell that her real feeling was one of having had a burden lifted from her. Her husband Herbert made no real attempt to hide his sense of relief, while the neighbours were enjoying the laying to rest of one of their number, and comfortably anticipating the tea to come.

The undertaker would obviously be happy, since it was a three-hearse job. The deceased woman had contributed to an insurance policy for the last forty years of her life, purely so that she could be laid to rest in what she had considered suitably impressive style. The fact that she wouldn't be there to witness her money being spent on it didn't seem to have detracted in any way from the importance she attached to the arrangement. Arnold, though, would personally have preferred that the money spent on the undertaker's men, walking solemnly and at a funereal pace in front of the hearse, had been put to some other use, since it slowed the procession to a crawl, and made the funeral seem to last an unconscionable time.

He didn't really know anything much else about the dead woman, Aggie Mulch, but judging by the perpetual griping she had gone in for while alive, whatever was in store for her was bound be to an improvement.

Arnold was a very serious little boy, so serious that he had no close friends of his own on the Estate. But then he had something to be serious about. He happened to possess an exceptional capacity for empathy, to the extent that he could practically experience what other people near him were feeling. Unfortunately, he also seemed to have little control over whether or no the faculty should come into play, for he had found, rather to his dismay, that if he was in sufficient proximity to someone who was in any sort of emotional state, his antennae would pick up the vibrations.

He couldn't remember when it was that he had first realised that this ability wasn't shared by others. For that matter, it was something that seemed to have gradually developed over the last few years. Up to the age of eight or nine, though he rather imagined he had always been more aware of his fellows than other children of his age, he had never been swamped by these perceptions in the way he often was nowadays.

When he finally had realised that he possessed a faculty not shared by his fellow humans, or at least none he had met or heard about, he had pondered long and hard about the wherefore of it. Why had he, Arnold Simpkins, on the face of it no one in particular, and whose parents were certainly nobody in particular, been selected as the recipient of this unusual ability?

He wasn't able to come to any conclusions; he just knew that it was up to him to use his gift for the benefit of society at large, though how was rather more of a problem. He could hardly just go up to people and offer to tell them how they felt, since they presumably already possessed this knowledge. On the other hand, the answers he had received to some of the naïve questions he had come out with, when he was first becoming aware of his extra perceptiveness, had made him realise that most people didn't realise how unhappy they were, and lots of them didn't even appreciate that they were unhappy at all.

So much misery was naturally distressing to poor Arnold, since he was able, even if only temporarily, to experience it for himself. But, he asked himself, what on earth could he do to save these poor creatures from an existence that so obviously wasn't worth while for them? Though he agonised over what he felt in some way was a responsibility laid on him, he couldn't come up with any practical answer. He mulled over all sorts of unsuitable and impractical ideas until, one day, the answer was laid before him, and he realised that he had indeed been called to a mission.

He had gone out of their thirteenth-floor flat to do some shopping for his mother, and he could hear Mrs. Pudgett across the floor shouting and screaming at her husband hysterically. She was, he already knew, a bad-tempered shrew, and gave her poor husband a hell of a time: it would be a good thing all round when she left this world of strife and sorrow. Arnold thought, with even more than his usual intensity, how much he wished he could help her to achieve such a worthwhile aim.

As the shouting increased, so did the strength of his sympathetic feeling, for he had stopped on the landing, as if paralysed by the human drama being enacted the other side of their door, albeit the fact that it was an oft-repeated one. Suddenly there was a heavy crash, and he heard Mr. Pudgett utter an exclamation that sounded to him like 'Omigawd.' Galvanised into life, he scuttled quickly down the stairs.

The next day he overheard his mother being told that Mrs. P., while in the middle of one of her frequent rows, had suddenly collapsed, and though her husband had dialled 999 promptly, by the time the ambulance arrived she was pronounced dead.

'How providential,' Arnold thought: that was one he need no longer worry about. But then he began to wonder. What had happened did seem a bit of a coincidence, he admitted to himself, and eventually there was nothing for it but that he must check his suspicions out.

First, though, he waited to hear what the doctor had to say. The official pronouncement turned out to be a cerebral embolism, and the doctor found nothing suspicious in the circumstances, so there wasn't even an inquest. That made it all the more necessary for him to find out if, in some unknown and mysterious way, he was connected with what had happened.

He felt a compelling need to attend the funeral: rather like a composer having his new work performed, or a playwright at the first night of a new play, he supposed. Unfortunately, by the time he had run there after he got out of school, it was all more or less over, and he felt distinctly cheated.

Who to choose for his little experiment was the next matter requiring urgent attention. Mentally running through a list of those of the inhabitants of the Estate that he knew personally, if not in any great depth, which was quite a large number for such a shy individual, he found himself spoilt for choice. With proper consideration for the seriousness of the selection process, he went through them systematically.

Should it be Mrs. Flaggle, confined to her bed by arthritis, whom nobody but the social worker went to see, because she was such a disagreeable old woman: Joe Smodd, who got drunk two or three times a week and would regularly beat up at least one member of his family on returning home: or Dick Wosker, one of the school bullies, who seemed to particularly have it in for Arnold, and was always pulling his hair, tripping him up, or finding some other way of making his time at school miserable.

Arnold's detestation of Dick was intensified by the fact that his parents were well-off, and seemed to keep him liberally supplied with pocket-money, whereas Arnold and his mother lived from hand to mouth, often having to wrap themselves in blankets because they couldn't afford to turn the electric fire on, and regularly in arrears with bills.

No: Arnold sternly repressed that thought. Motives of personal satisfaction must not in any way enter into his considerations. If he did indeed prove to possess some sort of gift of the kind, it must be used strictly for the benefit of society, not to indulge his own desire for revenge.

His weaker self argued back that Dick Wosker was an unpleasant character who bullied other small boys besides Arnold, so that removing him would be of general social benefit, but Arnold's conscience was firm. If he got any kind of personal advantage out of using his strange ability, it would, he felt, be tainted.

He went back to cataloguing the Estate, and before long felt certain he had lit on the right one: Mrs. Benzil, who lived in No. 174 with her daughter, and dominated her so totally that she had no life of her own, and was little more than her mother's skivvy. Everyone on the Estate agreed that it was high time Lizzie Benzil stood up to her or, better still, left the old bag to fend for herself, which she was perfectly capable of doing, and went off to try and build some sort of life apart from her, though at forty-two she'd probably missed the best part of it anyway.

Having made his decision, Arnold was eager to implement it. He pondered over the means. The Benzils lived in C block, where Arnold was not on visiting terms with anyone. He racked his brains to think of an excuse for being there, but couldn't come up with anything. Eventually he decided, in desperation, that he would just have to go there and risk being noticed. If he chose a time when Lizzie was out at work, the alarm would most likely not be raised until she got home, giving him a comfortable time margin. And anyway, who would connect his presence with the death of an old woman whose life in no way crossed his own?

He decided the best time was between when he got out of school, and before Lizzie got home from work. Luckily, at this time of year, it was already darkish at half-past four, and as it was also cold and windy, he didn't think anybody would be around to notice him enter C block. He avoided the lift, since if someone chose to use it at the same time, they would be certain to remember him.

When he got to the right floor, the eighth, he paused to get his breath back and then, no one being around, listened outside the door. He could hear footsteps and, a few moments later, the whistling of a kettle.

He still had no clear idea, at this stage, what were the means by which he had, if in fact he had, encompassed Mrs. B's demise, although he had thought it over a good deal. What he had decided to do, as a result of his cogitations, was concentrate on his chosen client, think about all the reasons why she would be better to depart this life, and then wish as strongly as he could to help her achieve this end. As far as he had been able to recall, that was all that he had done on the previous occasion, so it was obviously what he needed to check out.

Keeping an ear open for unwelcome arrivals, he concentrated as hard as he could. Nothing happened, as far as he could tell. After all his heart-searchings, he experienced a distinct feeling of anti-climax, and was on the point of giving up when he heard the sound of a cup falling on the floor and almost certainly breaking, then a heavier sound. He waited no further, but made himself scarce with all the speed at his disposal, and spent the rest of the evening reading quietly in the sitting-room, so as to make sure not to miss any snippet of information that might come his Mother's way.

But Mother, with the usual contrariness of parents, elected not to pop out for her usual cup of tea at her bosom friend Sarah's. This was frustrating for Arnold, since Sarah was one of the main reception and distribution posts for all the gossip of the Estate, and Arnold had been relying on this local version of the bush telegraph to get him stop-press information.

He knew his mother would find it slightly strange that he had elected to spend the evening in her company: normally he retired to his room with a couple of books. But he was burning with eagerness to know what, if anything, was the result of his little experiment. Not only that, but his Mother, having been told often enough by him that he was not interested in the goings-on of their neighbours, might not even bother to acquaint him with any news about Mrs. B. that might be going the rounds.

He stayed up as late as he could manage, but eventually had to retire with his curiosity entirely unsatisfied. He slept badly, but at least when he came down to breakfast the next morning, there was no chance of him missing the news: his mother was full of it. There had indeed been a death in the Benzil household: unfortunately, it was not old Mrs. B, but Lizzie.

Arnold was so taken aback by this information that his usual self-control quite left him, and he blurted out without thinking 'Lizzie? It can't be!'

Immediately it escaped his lips, he realised how incautious he had been, and racked his brains desperately for some cover-up line. Fortunately, his mother was too full of her own commentary to take any real notice, merely pausing in her retailing of a suitably and doubtless inaccurately embroidered version to tell him not to contradict his mother. Feigning suitable agreement, he listened avidly to her account.

Apparently old Mrs. B. had been taking her accustomed afternoon doze, and Lizzie, who had recently been put onto a twenty-five hour week and thus was usually home by three, was in the act of preparing the tea-tray, with which she customarily woke her mother up, when she had collapsed. With no one to wake her, Mrs. B. had gone on sleeping and not got up till early morning, when she had stumbled across Lizzie's body.

Arnold did not know what to think — or feel. On the one hand, it seemed his experiment had a successful outcome: on the other, it appeared that his talent, if that was what had been in action, needed a lot more careful handling than he had realised.

He did not waste too much energy regretting Lizzie's demise: her life had not been really worth living, anyway. However, it was obvious he was going to have to conduct any experiments much more rigorously if he was both to work out what it was he was able to do, and also keep it under proper control. But just then, with the maddening contrariness of fate, he developed a heavy cold, and when his mother found he had a temperature, he was packed off to bed in spite of his protestations, so he missed the funeral again.

With the single-mindedness of a true scientist, he didn't let this setback flummox him: he used his time in bed to draw up a list of people who would have no valid reason to object if he used them to verify just what he was capable of, and how.

This time, he knew, he needed to vary the type of subject. Reason and emotion came together perfectly in the shape of Dick Wosker. Most of the smaller boys at Arnold's school were frightened of him, and he had certainly used his superior bulk and strength to make Arnold's time at school an experience difficult to look forward to. Obviously a lot of youngsters would breathe a sigh of relief if some sort of termination to his existence could be arranged.

Being a very moral sort of person, Arnold understood that he must not choose Dick just out of personal motives; he must use the event to learn more, and thus justify the deed. While lying there he had plenty of time to think through various alternative strategies, and he realised that what he urgently needed was to actually see his power in operation. He racked his brains to think of a way to get Dick alone with him that didn't involve his being too frightened to be able to concentrate.

Eventually he decided it just wasn't practicable: any circumstance he could envisage with the two of them alone would probably result in his being in such a state that he wouldn't be able to use whatever ability he had efficiently. Then it struck him that, if he could manage to do it in the presence of a whole crowd of schoolchildren, that should prove a perfect alibi, and yet there was no reason why he shouldn't learn just as much as if the two of them were alone together.

In a couple of days he was well enough to go back to school, and when he arrived, looked around with a quite different sort of interest to see if Dick was about. There was no sign of him, and he sat tensely through Assembly, and the first two lessons before break, not really able to concentrate on what he was supposed to be doing.

However, Dick did finally arrive during break. It appeared he had been to the dentist: certainly he was in a more subdued mood than usual. Arnold sternly suppressed any feeling of common human sympathy, even though he dreaded the dentist himself, and, selecting a suitable moment, brought all his powers of concentration to bear on Dick as he held forth to a gang of cronies.

To his disgust nothing much happened: Dick did seem to turn pale for a moment and catch his breath, but almost immediately he was his old self again. Arnold was furious. Perhaps, he thought disconsolately, this meant that his powers would only work on the really old — people over forty, or even older. He felt very restricted: with natural human perversity he was unable to stop thinking of all those who didn't come into this category but nonetheless were, he was convinced, desperately unhappy, and so would have benefited from his help.

He walked round the playground kicking viciously at the base of the fencing that surrounded it. It was almost as though whatever had given him his special ability didn't trust him to use it carefully enough. He was being treated like a child, he felt, and it made him so furious that he almost vowed never to use it again.

In fact, he was upset enough that when the bell went, and he had to join the rush back to classes, he neglected his usual precautions, and found that he had ended up with Dick behind him. As it was French, and the French teacher was quite incapable of maintaining discipline, Dick was soon up to one of his favourite tricks, pulling hairs out of the back of his victim's head with a pair of tweezers.

This time, however, instead of cringing and crying as usual, Arnold turned round and gave his tormentor such a look of hatred that Dick was momentarily abashed, and dropped the tweezers. He bent to pick them up, and keeled over, his head hitting the floor with a loud crack.

Arnold hastily made himself look as inoffensive and innocent as possible, no difficult task with his slightly pasty features and large glasses, not to mention his small, rather dumpy frame. Matron soon arrived and organised the removal of Dick's limp frame, during which operation he kept well out of the way. When he heard later that the Doctor had pronounced Dick dead, he didn't know quite whether to be glad or sorry, since while he'd certainly managed another demonstration of what he could do, at the same time he was definitely right on the spot when it happened. If he appeared to be around at any further events of the kind, someone might start putting two and two together.

However, by the time a few days had passed, it was clear that no one had given the possibility of his being anything but an unwilling agent the slightest thought. At the inquest it was eventually decided that there had been an allergic reaction to the local anaesthetic administered by the dentist, and the verdict passed was 'death by misadventure.'

None the less, Arnold resolved to tread cautiously for the moment, though he didn't feel there was any need for him to cease his activities altogether. Dick's funeral, however, was rather a disappointment. To his amazement, quite a few of the mourners seemed genuinely upset. Arnold was very cross: it almost seemed as if they were criticising him.

He returned to his list in a distinctly bad temper. Further reconnaissance had enabled him to enlarge it considerably, and he almost began to quail at the magnitude of the task in front of him, and the responsibility laid on his small and none-too-broad shoulders.

Too many deaths of Senior Citizens on the one Estate, even if they earned him the gratitude of the Chancellor of the Exchequer, would be bound to arouse suspicion. And though he was pretty certain there was no way in which anyone could connect him to them, no trail which could possibly cause suspicions to be aroused about his possible part in the deaths, he knew it was his duty not to take any unnecessary risks or chances.

On the other hand, it would take him time to gather enough information about the inhabitants of other areas for him to be able to feel sure he was doing the right thing. Despatching someone who was still enjoying life would be a terrible mistake, which he must make every effort to avoid. And it was now February, which he had read somewhere was the time of year when people were at their weakest, and the highest number of deaths occurred, and so really the time when he should be busiest. On the other hand, he mustn't ever be as careless as he had been with Lizzie.

He decided to divide his list into urgent, and those who could wait. He would attend to the urgent cases, and then see how much furore was caused before he started on any of the rest. And finally he received the confirmation he had been waiting for, that his efforts were for the general good, when he attended the funeral of his next client, Mrs. Mulch, and found that just about everyone there was happy to be, so to speak, seeing her off.

His conscience refreshed, he went back to his task with renewed enthusiasm. The spate of deaths had received sufficient notice that the funerals were attended by a large number of the merely curious, so that nobody thought anything of his being present as well. Doubtless they would assume he shared their ghoulishness.

But when he returned home and saw his mother reading the local paper with the front page headline 'Mystery Killer,' he had a moment of total panic and fled to his room, where he sat trembling for quite a while. However, on finally descending and reading the item for himself, he found the suggestion was that some unknown virus was at the bottom of the wave of deaths of the aged and infirm.

Nonetheless, it partially destroyed his nerve, and he determined to lay off his activities until the scare had died down. Then fate took a hand: his great-aunt Millie invited them to stay with her for a holiday. His mother didn't much care for her, since she considered she gave herself airs.

Millie had married well during the War, and lived in a rambling ivy-clad house that fronted a broad river somewhere in the Midlands, Arnold couldn't remember where. But thinking that they would do well to temporarily abandon such a dangerous area, his mother swallowed her pride and accepted the invitation, upon which Millie sent them the train fare.

'Mum,' said Arnold as the train made its noisy way to their destination, 'are we visiting Aunt Millie for long?'

'Not long, just a few days. She can be very difficult.'

'But we're her only relatives since cousin Jessie died. Does that mean you're her heir?'

'I wouldn't worry about that, Arnold. Millie's fit as a flea. She's always boasting she's never had a day's illness,. If I had her money, I don't suppose I'd keep getting my turns,' his mother sighed.

'But you are her heir?'

"I wouldn't build your hopes up. Millie'll easily outlive me.' She smiled to stop him worrying about her.

Arnold smiled back.

GROUP READING

Quentin was at last coming to the end of the passage he had been reading, and as Simon glanced surreptitiously once more at their new member, or rather potential member, for he hadn't yet actually joined the group, he noticed that the fellow looked even more fidgety than when the reading had started. It reinforced the feeling he had had, when he first saw him: the crumpled jeans and check shirt hardly betokened literary abilities, and were distinctly at odds with the more decorous attire of the rest of the group.

On the other hand, they did suggest a more physical attitude to life than seemed to be the case with the other members, who didn't, up till then, include a single person with whom Simon could have contemplated any intimate contact, even in his usual fairly desperate state. He had hoped that, by moving to London, he would be able to get regular sex, or at least more regular than had been the case in Basildon, where his score averaged somewhere around three times a year. Unfortunately, being too shy to make friends easily or to go out cruising, and too fastidious to cottage, he found London little better, with the added irritation that he knew it was there all over the place, if only he could screw himself up to go out and get it.

But though he regularly promised himself he would, when it came to crunch time he always chickened out, so he did what he could to relieve his frustration by writing stories which, he assured himself, were erotic rather than pornographic, though even so it was an activity he made sure to keep entirely secret from the group. Admittedly he stayed faithful to the first principle he had imbibed from them, that there are no happy endings in anything with pretensions to being literature, so that the stories always ended, after an enthusiastic, if not very realistic, description of a sexual encounter, in the protagonist being left once more on his own, for one reason or another.

Simon viewed the newcomer — Godfrey had introduced him as Matt — with mixed feelings: he hardly seemed likely to fit in with the group, but on the other hand he was solidly built and could almost have come off a building site, so taking him near enough to the type of guy that peopled Simon's fantasies to set his pulse racing. There was an aura about him which suggested he got it regularly, too, he thought enviously, something that seemed highly unlikely with the other group members, who did their best to make it quite clear that they were only interested in the life of the mind. Though he strove mightily to emulate their example, Simon could not manage to expunge the constant stream of sexual thoughts and desires that tormented him, and which, at times like this, prevented him from concentrating properly on the literary feast being spread in front of him.

So he was guiltily conscious of some slight sympathy with Matt, especially as he himself experienced a considerable degree of difficulty in following Quentin's long sentences and somewhat convoluted style. He knew it was literature, so he persevered, but caught himself continually casting surreptitious glances at Matt, and even wondering what he liked doing, though each time he would redirect his attention to the reading with a mental slap.

When it finally stopped, the convener immediately rushed in with his judgment.

'Excellent, my dear Quentin,' he approved. 'I confess to having become a trifle apprehensive when I realised you were about to deal with the coarser side of life, but in the event you handled what could have been a distasteful subject without any taint of carnality, and I am sure no one could have taken offence.'

Simon was much the youngest of the group, and still rather over-awed by the high literary level of the other members, particularly Quentin, whose regular use of such terms as 'semiotics' and 'post-structuralist' made it clear to Simon that he operated at a stratospheric level which Simon himself was unlikely to ever attain. He racked his brains desperately for something intelligent to say about this latest offering, but as he hadn't even been able to work out why what Quentin had been describing merited such discretion, he felt at something of a disadvantage.

'Your similes were so well chosen,' Penelope, a long-standing woman member, remarked. 'I particularly liked the part where the butcher glances at him as he asks for half-a-pound of skinless sausages: that image will stay with me for a long time.'

'Skinless!' Terence rhapsodised. 'So subtle!'

'No one else could put so much meaning into a meaningless glance,' Claude enthused.

'Then the scene where he serves the sausages to Emily!' Miles was not to be outdone in appreciation. 'The underlying tensions were so brilliantly not expressed.'

'Your metaphoric deformations at the very end were simply superb' pronounced Jocelyn, who, by dint of having published a monograph on 'The aesthetics of the semi-colon' was their acknowledged literary expert. 'I fear the subtlety will be wasted on most readers, but even with the hoi polloi, it must make an effect on the subliminal level.'

'I didn't understand a word of it,' the new arrival, Matt, finally expostulated. The fact that his vowels betrayed his proletarian origins went some way towards explaining his obtuseness, though they could hardly excuse it. So there was an appalled silence at such crass insensitivity, while Miles thought to himself that it confirmed his impression that Godfrey had made an error of judgment in allowing him to attend their gathering.

'You might find it easier if you saw it on the printed page,' Clarence, more kind-hearted than the others, offered helpfully. 'I'm sure Quentin would be happy to lend you a copy.'

Quentin inclined his head gracefully.

Matt's outburst had caused Godfrey acute embarrassment. The convener was realising that he had should have checked the fellow's credentials more carefully before he allowed such an uncouth specimen to enter their little enclave, but on the phone the wretch had sounded perfectly acceptable to his sensitive ear, and when he had said that he was interested in the technique of fiction-writing, Godfrey had assumed a certain basic standard of culture. The fact that he had now revealed his proletarian status was hardly sufficient excuse to ask him to leave, so he overlooked his behaviour for the nonce, and called on Patrice to restore the tone of the meeting.

After a certain amount of searching among the masses of sheets in his folder, Patrice finally managed to extract what, he informed them, was the next chapter in the novel he was currently engaged on, and from which he had read sections at previous meetings.

'You will remember,' he began, 'that Julian has just been introduced to the new deacon, Basil Clanricarde, at a tea-party held to welcome him by the Vicar's wife, and finds something familiar about him. Then that evening he recalls why he thought he recognised him: he had once caught him cheating at Ludo when they were boys. We left him wrestling with his conscience over whether he should inform the Vicar. I take up the narrative at the point where —'

But it was all too much for the new arrival. 'What's gay about that?' he demanded truculently.

'I beg your pardon?' the Convener said a trifle coldly.

'This is supposed to be a gay writing group, isn't it?' Matt went on.

'The Convener inclined his head. 'It is,' he answered.

'Well, where's the gay bits?' the intruder wanted to know.

'What do you mean, gay bits?' the Convener asked, his tone growing more and more frosty by the second.

'You know what I mean, sport,' Matt said, compounding his offensiveness with an increasingly plebeian intonation. 'When do they have it off?'

'If you are referring to smut, that is not the sort of thing we encourage,' Godfrey said, his voice positively dripping ice.

'Not much point in my staying, then,' Matt declared, heaving himself up from the chair. 'Call yourselves gay writers! I reckon you got me here under false pretences.'

Everyone maintained a disapproving silence as he made his way to the door, dislodging several charming little pieces of North Korean Art Deco in the process, one of which didn't survive its journey.

Godfrey had been thinking of trying it at the Antiques Roadshow, but it was worth the loss to be rid of that crude fellow.

'What a disgusting brute,' Mervyn said, as they heard the front door slam. 'Does he imagine we have nothing better to do than pander to his vulgar cravings?'

'Perhaps now we can get back to literature,' Miles declaimed fervently.

There was a murmur of agreement round the room in which Simon joined abstractedly, after a last disappointed glance at the back of Matt's jeans. 'They might be very clever, but none of them has a rear view worth a damn,' he thought, with a flash of rebelliousness. But then his full attention was required to work out how to remove any carnal taint from the relationship between the protagonists in the story he had brought to read. It was perhaps fortunate that the discussion on some of the finer points arising from Mervyn's fascinating evocation of the spirit of the woodland, as seen from the point of view of one of the younger trees, a technical tour de force written entirely without the use of verbs, took up so much time that they didn't get round to his piece.

It was when he was walking home that Simon allowed himself to regret that they hadn't heard any of Matt's writing. It might have been quite amusing, he thought wistfully. Of course it was a literary group and not a pick-up joint, but he did wonder whether Matt would have extended him an invitation to come back for coffee, and he let his mind dwell on the possible consequences. Then, when he got home and was emptying his briefcase, he found a visiting card among the papers with the name Matthew Hutchings, and a phone number.

The fellow must have slipped it in as he left, he supposed: it was a nifty bit of sleight-of-hand, for he certainly hadn't seen it being done. He rather doubted if he could use it: should the group ever get to hear about it, they'd probably freeze him out. But it did start him off again, and soon he was seated at his word-processor, letting his imagination run riot. 'This one,' he thought, 'is going to be really steamy.'

And indeed it was: he became so over-heated that he had three wanks over the scenes conjured up, only finishing it by working on into the small hours. Lying there after he had switched off his computer, he reflected that there probably wouldn't be much point in actually contacting Matt now: after the degree of excitement his imagination had engendered, any actual encounter that took place couldn't possibly come anywhere near it.

MEMORIES

The whole thing is so appalling that I don't really know what to think about it. I can't say I feel any better for having found it all out, except that I now have the satisfaction, if that's the right word, of understanding just why I feel so miserable. But somehow knowing the cause doesn't seem to have improved my state of mind at all: I'm just as depressed as I was before I went to see him — my counsellor, I mean — only now I feel angry as well, and I have the burden of this terrible knowledge hanging over me.

I suppose, considering what it is that he's helped me dredge up, it's no wonder that I feel so dreadful. And of course, now that I've remembered what my father did to me when I was a defenceless little girl, I can't possibly feel the same towards him as I used to — well, I mean how could I? But, unfortunately, my mother flatly refuses to believe that what I've remembered is true, even though I can now recall the actual details of what went on: she declares it's quite impossible, and that I must be making it up. Of course, in a way I admire her for sticking up for her husband; at the same time it's quite awful that she can believe her own daughter would say these things about her father if they weren't true.

I admit it took me a long time to finally remember them, though: something like eight or ten months since I first went to see Michael — he's my counsellor. On my first visit, he just asked me, very sympathetically, what was the problem, and then listened while I tried to tell him how I was feeling, which was generally depressed, and finding life difficult to cope with.

He let me go on for quite a while, and all he said at first was 'It sounds to me as if the cause of your difficulties could go back quite a long way.'

At this stage I didn't even realise they had a cause; I thought it was something that had just happened to me, so naturally I pricked up my ears. When he went on to ask me all sorts of questions about my early life, I didn't hold anything much back, because I already had the feeling that I could trust him. Even though the questions got quite personal, I was able to answer them pretty truthfully, but then of course talking to him is the same sort of thing as talking to a doctor.

Anyway, that was it for my first session, but the next time I went to see him, he said to me 'I suspect that the root cause of your problem is that you were sexually abused when you were very young.'

I almost laughed at first, the idea seemed so ridiculous. Certainly I had no notion that anything of that sort had ever happened to me, and so I said to him quite definitely 'My parents weren't like that at all. Mother was too busy with her Women's Institute — she was the Secretary — to have that much time for us when we were kids, and my father was more interested in my brother than me. In fact, I remember being quite jealous of him because of this.'

But then he explained to me 'That could be a false memory, unconsciously invented by you, to allow you to shut away the trauma of what really happened.'

Well, I listened to him with respect, because after all he is a trained professional, and also he was the only person who had taken my problems really seriously, even seeming to think he could do something about them. But the idea still seemed quite preposterous, so I said to him

'How is it that, if what you're suggesting did happen, I've absolutely no recollection of it at all?'

Then he told me all about repression, and how when something happens to us that is too painful for us to bear, we shut it away, so that we aren't consciously aware of it any more.

'Unfortunately,' he went on, 'this repression doesn't actually seal it all off so that it's no longer a source of trouble. You still have bad feelings because of it, but now you don't understand where they come from.'

It was very interesting to have all this explained to me by an expert, but I still couldn't fit in what Michael was suggesting with what I knew of my father, and how I remembered him being when I was small. I said this to him — he's the sort of man you feel you can say anything to, and he won't get upset or snap at you — and he told me 'That is exactly how most people react when they're first confronted with the idea. But this is the conscious mind, trying to prevent its buried material from being brought back to surface awareness, because it's frightened that the pain you originally felt might be experienced once more, if you allow yourself to admit the truth.'

Even then, though he kept telling me that my troubles originated in the fact that I was abused when I was a little girl, I flatly refused to believe it: in fact, when I thought of my dad, it seemed a quite outrageous suggestion. However, I knew Michael had had a lot of experience with others who had similar difficulties to mine, and no one else was offering any help at all, so I continued going along for counselling. He kept working on me, and eventually, with the help of a number of sessions of hypnosis to uncover my repressed experiences, it began to come out.

I have to admit I am extremely disappointed that even having it all brought into the light of day hasn't made me feel any better: I still get these terrible depressions, and of course now I've no one to turn to but Michael, because I've broken off contact with my parents — well, actually it was they who broke it off with me, or, more specifically, my mother did.

When I told her what I'd discovered, she said 'You've invented the whole thing, you and that silly man you've been seeing, though I suppose he was the one who put the idea into your head in the first place. They're all the same, these psychiatrists, they've got minds like sinks.'

I explained to her quite quietly, considering, 'He's not a silly man, and he's a counsellor, not a psychiatrist.'

But it made no difference. 'They're just as bad,' she said dismissing the distinction as if it were of no importance. 'They're all obsessed with sex; they think it's at the bottom of everything. Well, I've lived with your father for nearly forty years, I know him better than anyone, and I think I'd have known if anything like that had gone on.'

Of course, what I wanted just then was to confront him with it, make him admit it, and tell him how he'd ruined my life, but she flatly refused to let me see him until, as she put it 'You've got all this nonsense out of your head.' Then she as good as turned me out of the house, so that I shouldn't be there when he came in. I expect you can understand how frustrated I felt: I went back to my little flat, where I shouted and screamed, and beat my head against the wall, but that didn't help me to feel any better. Even worse, it was another five days before I would be able to see Michael again: I phoned his number, but there was no answer, so I went round to see my brother.

I can't say he looked particularly pleased to see me, but then he's always been a selfish type, wrapped up in his own affairs, and not much interested in other people's. Still, he did ask me in, and I told him all about it, and how Mother had reacted. He was pretty unsympathetic and, without going so far as to call me a liar, said 'I can't say I ever noticed any sign of anything of that sort when we were kids. I know he used to go to a sauna and massage establishment, because he told me about it when I was eighteen or so, and finally came out to him about being gay. He was ever so much more relaxed about it than I'd expected, and I think it was to try and help me feel at ease that he mentioned then that he'd been going to this place for years, and it had kept him on the rails, because Mother wasn't really very interested in sex.'

I was quite shocked when he told me that about Father, but then I realised that, if he was the sort of man whose sexual lusts led him into something like that, then it was even more likely that he would also be the sort who could abuse his daughter.

I said that to Brian, but he just laughed at me and said 'I rather think the massage parlour was quite enough to keep dad going. He was much more interested in his fishing, as I know only too well, because he kept dragging me along with him. And I can assure you that it was just fishing.'

His flippant attitude really annoyed me, and I snapped 'You'd be the last person to know what was going on: you always had your head buried in some book.'

'Enjoying reading doesn't have to mean that you're totally cut off from what's going on around you' he retorted. And then, although he must have known I needed to talk about it with someone, he said that his boy-friend was due there any minute, and they were going off to inspect some house they were thinking of buying together.

I offered to go with them, but he said he didn't think it would be a good idea. So I realised it was just an excuse to get rid of me, and no doubt they didn't want me there because they were really planning to get up to whatever it is that two men get up to together. It's well-known all gay men are sex-mad.

Just to put the cap on it, he said as I was leaving 'I'm not at all sure this fellow you're seeing is good for you. You seem to be, if anything, rather worse than when you started these visits.'

That was absolutely too much, and I exploded. Michael has been absolutely wonderful to me, and I don't know what I'd have done without him. I must have tried his patience considerably in the early days of my counselling sessions, because I resisted what he was suggesting for a long time, with what now seems a ridiculous degree of stubbornness.

Luckily for me, he understood the situation, but then of course the experience he's had of similar cases to mine would have enabled him to feel certain that he had diagnosed the source of my problems correctly. So he persisted, and as I've said it gradually began to come out, until now I can remember it all very clearly. I tried to tell that to my dear brother, but he wasn't interested. I suppose that being gay makes you unable to understand the problems of normal people.

The next time I saw Michael, and he asked me how I was getting on, I told him about how cut-off I was feeling, and he put me in touch with a group called SOA, Survivors Of Abuse, so I went along to some of their meetings. At least there everybody knew what it felt like to have been abused, and treated it with proper seriousness, though I was more comfortable with those like me, who'd had these memories dredged up from where they'd originally been hidden.

Those who'd never repressed it, living with the knowledge all their lives, but for some reason not feeling able to talk about it until recently, made up their own little clique, and didn't seem very interested in the rest of us. But at least no one was likely to call you a liar, or suggest you'd made it all up, which I know is what my family and their friends are thinking. Unfortunately, because of my problems, I've never had the chance to make friends of my own, so there wasn't anyone else to turn to.

Even so, eventually I stopped going to the meetings except very occasionally because, for one thing, they weren't a very cheerful collection. I couldn't help noticing that having these repressed memories brought out didn't seem to have made any of us any happier. Lots of them were still extremely angry, and of course there were a number who'd insisted on bringing the police into it, and preferring charges against the parent responsible

The main reason I stopped going, though, was because they began to make me wish Michael had never started on me. I know I would still have been unhappy, of course, but now I'm unhappy and I also have this dreadful knowledge that I can't really come to terms with. I suppose that's why a number of those who had belonged to the group also dropped out, though I heard that some of them had actually rejected their uncovered memories, deciding the whole thing was imaginary.

I suppose that's actually quite understandable: the pressure they experience, and I know only too well for myself how heavy that is, made them feel their recovered knowledge was too much to bear, and so they rejected it. I have to admit there are times when I wish I could do the same thing myself, but now that I've remembered it all, I don't think I'll ever be able to forget it, or the dreadful effect realising it had on me

Michael says I'll soon start feeling better, but I'm still waiting for that to happen. I just have to hold on to the belief that he knows what he's taking about.

PERSONAL COLUMN

Every few months, I have observed without pleasure, I find myself needing the kind of physical relief that one can only get from contact with other people. Most of the time it's a simple enough matter to defuse that sort of charge by oneself, but the human animal unfortunately seems to retain enough of its primitive heritage to need this physical interplay at least occasionally, and I find that, if I do nothing to supply the need, I am in a fidgety and irritable mood for a period of several days, occasionally even weeks.

Perhaps this might provide some support for the bio-rhythm hypothesis, I don't know, but anyway it is a damn nuisance. Last time it happened to me, I determined that, when it recurred, I would do something about it immediately, rather than wasting several days in this state of restless frustration.

I had found out, after a series of observations, and through recourse to my diary, that this was liable to happen about twice a year, at more or less the same time each year, a circumstance in itself worthy of some investigation, when I should have the time and attention to spare. But more immediately pressing was to 'blow the charge,' to use the vernacular, at as early a stage as possible, and thus be able to get back to my work with the minimum of interruption.

With this in mind, I placed an advertisement in the personal columns of one of the gay papers couched, I hoped, in sufficiently interesting terms to attract a reasonable number of responses. I allowed myself a certain amount of poetic license in framing the wording but, after scanning a number of other advertisements beforehand, I was fairly certain that all the other advertisers had, so to speak, adulterated their copy in the same way.

Obviously it would not be sensible to exaggerate too much, otherwise the disparity between the advert and the reality might work against the achievement of my object, so I was careful to avoid superlatives, and eventually I worked out the ad below :

'Attractive intelligent tall slim young guy, sincere, seeks similar for hopefully long-term commitment'

I was quite pleased with it when I finally sat back and read it through. Okay, admittedly I had shaded the truth in one or two aspects, but then, as I said, I felt reasonably certain everybody else was doing the same. I made sure, though, not to show it to any of my closer acquaintances, since I knew their comments would be unkind, not to say ribald.

I put it in for two weeks, since even if I got more suitable replies than I needed at this time, I reasoned that one or other of them might well come in handy on the next occasion I should be feeling in this sort of mood. Then I sat back to await the deluge of letters.

I don't know where I'd gone wrong in my phrasing, but it was more of a trickle than a downpour. In the first week there was nothing, but I believe that's quite common, as the rags take some time to circulate round, and answering personal ads seems to be for many people quite a leisurely business. But at least in the following week I got six. I tipped all the replies out, slit open the envelopes, and sat back to read them.

The first one I opened was from Berkshire, in fact the other side of Reading, too far for me to bother. This in spite of the fact that my advert had appeared in a magazine which was specifically for Londoners, so that neither I nor most of the other advertisers had bothered to include the word 'London' in our ads. The passport-photo type of snap he enclosed did nothing to change my mind, either.

Nor was the next reply calculated to increase my adrenaline output. Written in pencil on about six lines-worth cut off a standard A4 sheet, the sender had obviously not bothered to consider the effect his communication might have on its recipient, which in itself was a bad sign, and then he hadn't enclosed a photo at all, which I did not find encouraging, to say the least.

So now it was two down and four to go, and my excitement was already considerably diminished by the time I got to the third reply. This was written on paper of a fairly deep yellow hue, and enclosed in an envelope of the same sort of paper, so I expected the worst, but the contents did allay my fears to some extent, since they were neatly typed and forthright without being vulgar, while the snapshot enclosed showed someone quite presentable, though without being in any way striking.

I filed that one under possibles, and the next one also went into the same pile, largely on the strength of the photo he'd enclosed, which was perhaps a trifle bold, but did manage to raise my pulse-rate a few degrees. Numbers five and six, however, were both no-nos, one of them couched in language so coarse that I knew at once we would have nothing in common, while the other went to the opposite extreme, displaying an obvious yearning for romance, which I felt would make the achieving of my purpose just too much hard work.

So I rang up number three, whose name was John, and arranged to meet him at nine o'clock the following Friday, in a pub that was vaguely equidistant from our respective abodes. I already had a photo by which to recognise him, of course, and in addition he had told me what he would be wearing. I in return gave him the same sort of information, but when the time came for me to go, I deliberately altered my attire sufficiently so that, if I decided not to follow through, he wouldn't be able to feel sure of recognising me, and so inhibit my getaway.

I arrived well before the agreed time, largely so as to get a seat at the back of the room, something usually in short supply, since this would enable me to take a good look at him without being too visible. Then, if I did decide I didn't want to make contact, I could still preserve my anonymity.

He arrived more or less at the time agreed, and I was easily able to spot him making his way through the crowd to the bar. It wasn't until he had finally managed to get himself a drink that he turned round, and started scanning the various faces. It was just as well that he'd told me what he'd be wearing, since I doubt if I would have been able to be confident about recognising him from the photograph he had sent. Watching him in action as he threaded his way through the crowd, though of course without letting him notice that I was looking at him, I couldn't decide whether I fancied him at all or no.

The casual gear he had adopted made it plain that he had quite a reasonable body: on the other hand there seemed something a bit aggressive about his manner, a hint of impatience and irritability that I thought I would find uncongenial. I couldn't make up my mind whether or no I wished to follow up the contact, but while I was hesitating he meanwhile was looking over the whole assembly, and of course he saw me as well, though without realising that I was the one he was supposed to meet, since, as I said, I had misled him about what I would be wearing, and of course he had never seen a photo of me.

Unfortunately, by the time I had decided that it could be interesting, he would have seen me sitting there and so my little ruse would be exposed. I thought that would be bound to start us off on a bad footing, so I had to pretend I hadn't gone there to meet him.

Eventually, after about an hour, he gave up and left, after which I went home, determined to be a bit more decisive next time. Fortunately there still was number four to try. He'd given a phone number, so I rang him up, and I quite liked the sound of his voice when he answered, pleasantly masculine and decisive without being too much so.

He sounded really keen for us to meet, and suggested I should go round to his place, and I thought I'd better, so we fixed up a date just a couple of days hence. He gave me his address, and I said I'd phone him before I left just to confirm I was on my way, managing to ring off without having had to give him my phone number or address, which of course was a bit of a relief.

When the time came, I spruced myself up a bit, though not enough to make it look as if I was desperate, rang him as I'd promised, and off I went. Unfortunately, when I saw him, I couldn't really say he did anything much for me, and I fell to wondering what it was about his photo that had got me thinking he might.

Of course I didn't show that I was a bit disappointed; we had a drink and chatted, and eventually he suggested we should go into the bedroom. I agreed with my best shot at showing enthusiasm, so off we trooped, but I can't say it was a great success. For a start, I thought he was a bit uninhibited with someone he'd only met a few minutes before, and the sort of activities he seemed to want to indulge in were not the kind of thing I would allow myself to join in with any Tom, Dick, or Harry.

In my opinion, his approach displayed a certain lack of realism: it should have been perfectly obvious to him from the word go that we were only consorting for the purpose of mutual physical relief, not to indulge in intimate acrobatics. I fear he was a little disappointed when I refused to indulge his wilder flights of fancy, but really there are limits to what one is prepared to get up to with semi-strangers, and the fact that he didn't appreciate this made it clear to me that he had a rather indiscriminate approach to such matters, which did not encourage me to pursue the contact any further.

All in all the session was not a great success, but on the other hand I found, with a good deal of relief, that it had satisfactorily removed the pressure I was under, so that I was able once more to get back to less bothersome pursuits.

THE PRIZE

Usually the only time I buy raffle tickets is when, for one reason or another, usually just plain cowardice, I can't manage to say 'No' to whoever it is that's trying to persuade me to buy them. Okay, that's most of the time, but certainly I don't buy them in the expectation or even hope of winning a prize, and to date that's how it's been.

But this last one, which I actually bought because I felt I ought to support the cause, proved to be an exception. I hadn't stayed for the draw: usually an hour or so is all that I can stand at these functions, especially as I am pretty useless in the chatting-up stakes, and at my age, with middle-aged spread declaring itself more obviously day by day, I don't expect anyone's fancy to light on me.

So I forgot about my raffle ticket until I got a letter through the post, telling me I'd won third prize, which turned out to be an evening with an escort named Bob. My immediate reaction was to feel slightly threatened, which a moment's cool reflection soon dispelled, but though, of course, there was a little frisson of excitement, that was more than counter-balanced by all sorts of doubts.

For a start, I'd never used that kind of service. I suppose I'm as interested in sex as the next guy, which means I spend a lot of time chasing it and then, on the occasions when the hunt is successful, finding that the reality doesn't measure up to the fantasy. I've had a few affairs as well, none of them madly passionate or, it seems now when I look back on them, particularly successful, but with them there was always something getting in the way of simple sexual pleasure. I guess it was mostly that for some reason we were too inhibited to sort out the little matter of mutual satisfaction.

As I said, I'm not good at chatting up, for which reason I prefer to use cottages, and so, when the urge gets too strong, I go off to one of these, where I score with reasonable frequency. I don't know if it's me getting picky, or the fact that the guys available to me at my present age are nothing special, or that I don't come over as interesting or sexy enough to attract the better ones, but I usually end up feeling I'd have done better to stay home and have a wank.

Even so, the thought of paying somebody for sex had never seriously occurred to me. I suppose I thought that it was for the old and desperate, and I hadn't got round to classifying myself that way yet. Of course, I'd come across a few youngsters, or comparative youngsters, while cottaging, who'd asked for money, or offered to come back with me for it, but I'd never taken them up on their offers. In fact, it had been an instant turn-off, especially as none of them looked anything to write home about anyway.

But eventually, I plucked up my courage and phoned the number on the card. The first time all I got was his answer-phone, but I didn't leave a message, just rang off, and tried again the next evening. This time I was luckier, and when I'd established that I was talking to the correct guy, I explained that I had won the prize of an evening with him.

He chuckled, and said 'Hey, that's great: I've been waiting for you to phone. When do you want to come round?'

I suppose I'm a bit cautious by nature: anyway, I wanted to establish that I wouldn't be forced into anything I didn't want to do, so I said 'I think I ought to explain that I've never visited an escort before, and ..'

I was hesitating over what to say next when he interrupted with 'That's no problem: everyone has to make a start sometime. I'll do my best to see you get a good introduction to the service.'

I was still stammering a bit, but I went on determinedly 'I might not want to...' trailing off delicately.

'You don't need to worry about that,' he assured me confidently. 'The customer is always right. Do you want to know a bit about me before we meet?

'Yes, that would be nice,' I replied, cursing myself afterwards for sounding so inane.

But he didn't seem to notice, just described himself so fluently that it was obvious he'd done it many times before.

'I'm five foot ten,' he announced, ' and quite solidly built. I'm sun-tanned all over, fair with short cropped hair and blue eyes, quite nice-looking, and I've got an eight-inch cock, pretty thick.'

I'm not really used to that degree of blatancy in conversation, so I stumbled for words for a few moments before I managed to get out 'That sounds very interesting.'

'What about you?' he asked. "Do you want to tell me a bit about what you're like?'

'I'm afraid you won't find me anything much,' I rather mumbled, a bit embarrassed. 'I'm forty-six, nothing special in the looks department, and going out of shape rather faster than I would wish.'

'Don't put yourself down,' he chided me. 'I like the sound of your voice, and I'm sure we'll get on together. When do you want to come over?'

We settled on the evening of the coming Friday, and I rang off. Then, of course, I thought of all the questions I should have asked while I had the chance. I had no real idea what to expect, or even whether there would be any sex involved, though the fact that he'd mentioned his cock made me think there would. But I'd no idea what he was into sexually, for instance: we could be totally incompatible

I have to admit that, in spite of still feeling somewhat dubious about the whole thing, and constantly reminding myself not to build it up too much, since it could be a prize fiasco, I spent much of the rest of the week wondering what the encounter was going to be like. When Friday evening finally arrived, I got ready as if I was going to a real date: had a bath, cleaned my teeth, and generally did everything I could think off to make myself look as presentable as possible.

He had offered me the option of my visiting him, or him coming round to my place, and I decided I'd rather he didn't know where I lived, so I went to his flat. It was reasonably central, and prompt on eight o'clock I was ringing his bell. I don't know what I'd been expecting, but when he opened the door and let me in, although he was as he'd described, nonetheless I must confess to feeling something of a disappointment. I suppose I'd rather envisaged someone with modelly looks, but he was really quite ordinary: pleasant enough, but not in any way striking.

I trust I managed to hide any disappointment I was feeling, following him into quite a reasonable flat, comfortable enough if not exactly luxurious, and I thought to myself 'Perhaps he doesn't make as much money as I thought.' He offered me a drink, and as I wanted to keep all my wits about me, I opted for coffee.

While he was making it, I looked around the flat, but there was nothing of what I'd expected: no erotic pictures on the walls, no signs of his trade; he could have been a bank-clerk for all I could see. It was something of an anti-climax, but very soon he had brought me my coffee, after which he sat down in an easy chair near me and started chatting.

Of course I realised it must be an act, but he really sounded as if he was interested in me and my admittedly rather dull life. To my surprise, I found that, before very long, I was chatting away to him quite freely, so that instead of sitting there rather straight with my legs crossed, as I normally do with strangers, I had relaxed, and was leaning back on the sofa as if I'd known him for some time.

We must have been chatting for quite a while, and I was enjoying his company, when he asked me if I'd like him to give me a massage. I tensed up a bit when he suggested it, but I immediately reminded myself that I'd be a laughing-stock if my friends heard that I'd visited an escort and come away without having anything in that line, so I said 'Yes, thank you,' and he led me into the bedroom, where there was a fair-sized double bed. He laid a towel across it, told me to strip off and lie on it face down, then went out and left me to get on with it.

I undressed rather slowly, because, though I know it sounds ridiculous, I felt almost as if I were on trial. I folded my clothes neatly and lay them on a chair, then I lay down as instructed, and closed my eyes. Shortly I felt him come back into the room, and then he dripped some oil on my back and started to massage me. It was all perfectly straightforward and above-board at first, and after a little while I felt quite relaxed and was enjoying the sensation of his hands working my body over.

Occasionally they hands strayed near the more sensitive areas, but they never remained there, and by the time this had happened a dozen or so times, I found myself rather wishing that they would.

He worked on my neck and my shoulders, then moved onto my legs, and it must have been quite some while later that I felt him gently stroking my balls. It was very exciting, and I got an instant hard-on. He continued for a while, then moved up to my cleft and stroked there gently. I found myself holding my breath, because it was intensely stimulating. A few moments and a dab of some lubricant later, he was gently attempting to insert his finger.

I don't get fucked nowadays for the obvious reasons, not that when it did happen years ago I ever found it particularly interesting. I would just let it happen to oblige whoever I happened to be with, if that was what they wanted. So I tensed up as soon as he tried, but he whispered to me not to worry, just relax, nothing would happen that I didn't like, and I felt I could trust him, so I let him continue. He probably thought I was quite used to getting fucked, though actually any looseness there was due to the dildo I use sometimes when I'm feeling horny and can't be bothered to go out, or haven't had any luck when I do.

But he came over as a genuinely nice guy, added to which I didn't have the feeling with him that I've always had with others, that they're expecting something from me, and it's up to me to supply it. For a change it actually seemed as if he was more interested in giving me what I wanted than attending to his own needs, so I rather abandoned myself to what he was doing. He kept going gently without any attempt to rush anything, and I found myself getting hotter and hotter, till eventually I was moving around in response to what he was doing, even making little moans of appreciation.

It was so unlike me I was amazed at the back of my mind; at the same time I was enjoying myself so much I didn't bother with those or any other thoughts, I just concentrated on what he was doing to me. By this time I knew I really wanted him to fuck me. I wanted his dick more than I could ever remember wanting a dick before, and when he whispered 'Would you like me to fuck you?' I just nodded.

He gave me a bottle of poppers to sniff, and I unscrewed the top ready. I'm ashamed to say I don't think I'd have stopped him if he hadn't used a condom, but as it was I heard him open the packet and roll one on, in an obviously well-practised way. Then he got on top of me and slipped inside very gently and slowly. I took a deep sniff from the bottle in case, though he was so controlled I don't think it would have hurt even without it, and when he was right in and lying on top of me, I felt a deep satisfaction.

I expect you've had the experience of eating at some establishment where the chef is a real artist. You order some dish you know well, then you taste what he serves up, and you realise you've never really eaten it before; the others were pale imitations of the real thing. That's exactly what it felt like when he got fucking me. He started off in a very relaxed sort of way, quite short strokes, not at all like the sort of thing that had happened to me before, and gradually he used more and more of the full length of his dick till he was taking it almost completely out before sliding back in, all the time supporting the weight of his body on his hands.

It wasn't like sex, or anyway the sort of sex I was used to, cos there was no urgency about it, no sense of aiming for climax, but it was incredibly exciting all the same. Instead of all the movements blurring into one crude sensation, each in and each out stroke produced its own individual thrill, immediately followed by another, until eventually I was just lying there, conscious of nothing but the effect he was having on me.

I have absolutely no idea how long he went on like this, because I really lost all sense of time, but after a bit he lowered himself down onto me and fucked me gently while he stuck his tongue in my ear and licked my neck. It was almost too much, and I felt myself moaning as I quivered in the intensity of what I was experiencing, Then he started increasing the pressure a bit, fucking me harder, and from pure physical instinct I gripped his dick tightly and responded to each stroke as if to the manner born, though it was something I'd never even thought of doing with anyone else.

But after a bit he pulled out and got off me, while I waited passively for what he had in mind. I was told to turn over, then he got hold of my legs and pulled me to the edge of the bed. Then he stood at the end of the bed, held my legs up and entered me while he was standing. Soon we were away again, only this time he seemed to penetrate deeper, which was even more exciting.

I was moaning away, saying all sorts of things I'd never thought to hear myself saying, and which I could never have brought out in cold blood, till eventually, as the pace hotted up still further and his fucking got more urgent, I surpassed myself by calling out 'Come up me, baby,' which I'd never in a million years thought to hear myself say, especially as I'd only been having safe, not to say ultra-safe, sex for the last dozen or so years.

Anyway, when I came out with that, he turned me over onto my tummy again, still over the bed, and then lowered his head until he was kissing and licking me again, interspersing it with 'You're a really great fuck,' and more comments along those lines. I was doing my share of the work, almost automatically though with great enthusiasm, and eventually he gasped 'I'm going to come,' and a few seconds later I felt his whole body quiver in a really heavy orgasm.

He lay there for just a moment, then slid his dick out and got off me, while I turned over to look at him. He'd already taken the condom off and, as soon as he'd disposed of it, he said 'I'm just going to take a quick shower' and I heard the water running. But only a couple of minutes later he came back in, towelling himself, and then he lay down beside me. I turned to him and whispered 'I rather think you already know that you've just given me the best fucking of my life.'

He laughed, then after a bit he asked me 'Do you want to come off?' and the strange thing was that I didn't. I'd had a hard-on all the time he was fucking me, but as soon as he'd come it subsided, and I felt fully satisfied without that sort of climax. I told him no, he'd quite worn me out, and he laughed again. I wanted to kiss his body, but I didn't because I thought that, now he'd come off, he'd be feeling rather different, even though he seemed to be lying there very companionably. But anyway after a bit he said 'How about another coffee?' and I said 'That would be nice' so he got up, pulled on a dressing-gown, and made us both a cup.

I expect you can imagine the strange mixture of thoughts that was going through my head. On the one hand, I was appalled to think it had taken until I was forty-six to find out what sex was about: on the other, I was pretty certain, judging from all the other guys I'd had trade with, that they hadn't known any more about it than I had and that, unless someone awoke them the way I'd been woken, they would go to their graves not knowing. Even if it never happened again, I felt I understood what ecstasy was for the first time, and I experienced a surge of gratitude towards Bob for having shown me, though at the same time it was a real let-down to know I was just a job to him, and that it wasn't going to lead anywhere.

I put these thoughts to one side as he came back with our coffees and, because I was viewing him quite differently from before our little session, I started asking him about himself. He wasn't very expansive in that area, remarking only that his background was pretty dull and ordinary. He added that he'd just drifted into escort work, but had no plans to do anything else for the present.

I was enjoying myself a lot more than usual, but all the time at the back of my mind was the depressing thought that here was somebody I would have loved to have as a lover or even friend, but to him I was merely a client. I'd already asked him how much he charged, and when he told me, it sounded an extremely reasonable amount, and I said so. But then he grinned and explained that he'd quoted his standard one-hour rate, and that if a punter wanted the whole evening, or an all-nighter, the fee went up considerably. That was a bit of a downer: I realised that my prize had been rather more valuable than I'd imagined. I couldn't see myself spending that sort of money on my salary, and after what I assumed had been the de-luxe treatment, I felt it would be too much of an anti-climax to downgrade myself to the level of ordinary punter.

But I didn't want to spoil what time I had left with him, so I put that thought to the back of my mind, and changed the subject by remarking how odd I thought it that I hadn't wanted to reach a climax myself. He told me, though, that this was quite common with clients who were seriously into being screwed, and I wondered if, because the sensations are experienced through your arse, that becomes the centre of interest, and one's cock takes a back seat, so to speak.

'I suppose you've been fucked a lot?,' he asked me, and I answered 'No, hardly at all.' In fact, I've never been into fucking much, though I've always been the active partner since the scare started. In case he didn't believe me, I added that I did have a couple of dildos I used occasionally. Probably because of how easily I'd been able to take him, he seemed quite surprised at this: anyway he asked me 'Do you prefer giving it, then?' and because I felt so in tune with him I admitted that I'd never got an awful lot out of that either, and that what he'd just done to me was in a totally different league.

'You seemed like a natural to me,' he said thoughtfully. 'I really enjoyed fucking you, and that's no bullshit.'

Of course I felt a warm glow when he said that, but I couldn't think of any suitable answer, so I just finished my coffee. Then I started to get up and said 'I suppose I ought to be going,' but he said 'You don't need to go unless you want to. I haven't got anything planned for the rest of the evening.'

I certainly hadn't anything particular to go home to, so I sat down again and we continued chatting. I was, I must say, quite surprised to find that he actually seemed to be enjoying my company, and it made me a bit bolder than I usually am, so I asked him all sorts of questions about his work, which he answered, I imagine, perfectly frankly. From what he said, it turned out to be quite different to the fantasy picture I'd built up beforehand, much more boring than I could have imagined, but he seemed perfectly happy doing it.

We chatted quite a bit longer, and it was with a real feeling of regret that I finally got up and left. As I made my way home, I couldn't help thinking how well we'd got on, and that there must be something at least slightly special between us, which would only be spoilt if I ever saw him again on a more ordinary basis. I decided that I would certainly want to use escorts again, but I'd be better to forget him, and look out for somebody else from among the hundreds who offer themselves with various degrees of blatancy.

Of course I was just being over-romantic, a weakness I admit I'm prone to on occasions, and it wasn't that long before I phoned him up and arranged to go round like any other client. I was a bit apprehensive when I went round there that, because I was now just an ordinary punter, unable to afford the de-luxe treatment, the visit would be a disappointment, but in fact he did seem really pleased to see me. He kissed me as he opened the door, and then when I was inside said 'It's good too see you again.'

He made me a coffee, and we had a bit of a chat, before he suggested we got down to it, and then he repeated the same sort of scenario, only this time there was only a few minutes of massage before he got down to the sex. But I didn't mind that, because I'd been reliving that first time in my mind, so that my body was already warmed up and ready, and the fucking itself was still pretty wonderful, even if not quite as exciting as the first time. I didn't want to overstay my welcome, as the last thing I wanted him to think was that I was presuming on a friendship that didn't really exist, but he made me another coffee, and we had quite a chat before I finally went.

Now, of course, visiting him has become an important part of my life: in fact, if I'm totally honest, I suppose my visit to him is pretty well the centre-piece of my week. If I had that sort of money, I imagine I'd suggest he came to live with me, though I've a feeling he values his independence too much to enjoy being a kept boy. I'd like to take him out to dinner or the theatre before we got down to the other, but I feel a bit embarrassed about suggesting it. I did ask him once whether he was interested in opera, but he didn't seem very keen, so I let it drop. The problem is, if I did ask him, he might expect his evening rate, and that would be too expensive for me, especially with the cost of the meal and the tickets on top. So I haven't pursued it, but I've promised myself that,when I get a decent raise, I'm going to treat myself, so at least I've got something to look forward to.

THE SEVENTH DOOR

I came to London without much forward planning, so to speak, and it was soon pretty obvious that, without a job, my savings, such as they were, wouldn't last very long. I kept applying for anything that looked remotely suitable, but without success; there was just too much competition, a lot of it more experienced than I was. So when I saw an ad in one of the gay papers offering free lodging in return for household duties, I was naturally interested, and wrote off to the box number address, though without much hope.

I got a reply asking me to phone and make an appointment, which I did immediately, and the man I spoke to made an arrangement to meet me in town. I was worried about missing him, but in the upshot there was no chance of that. He was unmistakable, dressed completely in black, with a thick head of hair, and a beard that matched the colour of his clothes quite closely, apart from a sort of metallic-blue sheen.

He took me into a cafe, ordered coffee, and while we drank that, asked me a number of questions about myself. When I told him that I had been forced to leave home when my parents found out that I was gay, and since had had no contact with them, he was very sympathetic, and asked if I didn't have any other relatives who were more kindly disposed. I told him the truth, that I'd decided I was well shot of the whole small-minded gaggle, and had cut myself off from them completely. He agreed that I'd made the right decision, and then, after a few more questions, abruptly offered me the position on a week's trial, to be extended if both parties found the arrangement satisfactory. Of course I jumped at it; he gave me the address, and it was fixed for me to move in on the following Sunday.

That was no big event, just me turning up with a couple of bags. He showed me what was to be my room: not particularly large, but large enough, and way above what I'd expected. Then he gave me a quick whisk round the rest of the house, after which he left me to sort myself out, saying that there'd be something to eat in half-an-hour or so.

When I came down, he produced a hot savoury and a bowl of salad, both from M & S — I found out later that cooking was a chore he hated — together with a glass of wine. When I'd finished that, he poured us some coffee, motioned for me to sit in one of the armchairs opposite him, and after a few pleasantries began to instruct me in my duties.

These were not excessive, and he was at pains to assure me that, apart from them, my life was my own to live as I chose. Practically the only stipulation he made was that I should not bring any strangers — presumably a euphemism for casual trade — to the house, and I thought I had finally fallen on my feet. I just hoped that I would prove satisfactory.

The seven days passed and it seemed I had acquitted myself satisfactorily, for the arrangement was made permanent. Often the only time we were together was at supper, which I would prepare and we would eat together — when he was around, that is, for after the trial period he was often absent, sometime just for the day, at other times for considerably longer periods.

When he was with me he was always polite and courteous, but a tad distant. He had a rather serious manner, in fact I practically never saw him smile, and when he did it was only for a moment. I got the impression he was either sad or unhappy, probably both, but I had no idea why, and his manner didn't encourage me to ask him any personal questions.

Although there was a large double bed in his bedroom, I never noticed him take any company into it. The house was a fair size but, as it was far from cluttered, keeping it in order was no particular effort. There was also what was presumably a large cellar, but the only part of it I ever saw was some kind of anteroom all done in white, except for another door leading off it which was painted in a mixture of light and dark blue. This, though, was locked, and none of the keys on the key-ring he'd given me fitted it.

Of course I was curious about what was locked away there that he wanted to keep hidden from me, but he wasn't the sort of person you could ask. Very occasionally, late at night, I would hear him go down there with someone, but I never heard them come out, so no doubt whatever went on continued well past the time when I'd gone to sleep.

Strangely enough, he always seemed even more taciturn the morning after these occasions, and of course that made me more curious about what he got up to. But although he'd begun to unbend with me, and sometimes would join me in the sitting-room when I was watching television or listening to the radio, I still knew practically nothing about him: I had no idea what he did for a living, for instance, though obviously it was something that didn't require him to keep regular hours, and any paperwork that might have given me a hint was no doubt securely locked away in the safe he kept in his bedroom.

Eventually I became a little bolder and, if he was still in the room when the particular programme I was watching finished, I would switch off the set and try to engage him in conversation. At first I was careful to confine it to impersonal things, and if we were talking about say, political issues in which he had an interest, he could get quite animated. Then, after a few weeks, I got to telling him a bit about myself and what I'd been doing, and he would listen, even appearing to be interested, but he never volunteered anything, either about his activities, or any ideas he might have for the future.

With no living expenses and a not ungenerous pocket-money allowance, I could afford to go out a couple of nights a week without any problem, and I soon became a lot more sophisticated so far as gay society and practices were concerned. But though of course I had a fair amount of sex as a result, which was enjoyable enough, it never superseded my interest, I could almost say fascination, with my employer, a tribute no doubt to the adage that everyone likes a mystery.

It was quite a few weeks, even so, before I summoned up the courage to try a few very general questions such as 'Did you have a good day today?,' but I received only the vaguest and most non-committal of replies, and a lesser man would no doubt have been discouraged. But by this time he'd definitely got me intrigued, and I was determined to get past the barrier sooner or later, by hook or by crook.

I had also learned by this time that I was not the first house-boy he'd taken on, even though there were absolutely no signs that anyone else had ever lived in the house, no photos, nothing that they might have left behind; it was almost as if they'd never existed. I wondered if it would be the same when I moved on. The thought was mildly depressing; I suppose no one likes to feel he's left no impress of any kind behind him. And certainly he never mentioned any of them, never even hinted that there'd been anyone before me, I only found out through one of the local shops, where the owner was something of a chatterbox.

In spite of his uncommunicativeness, I felt sure by this time that there was something going on between us, even if he wasn't prepared to acknowledge it openly. I took to wandering round the house wearing just a pair of trunks, and though he tried to hide his interest, I often caught his gaze on me. More surprising was the realisation that I was beginning to find him attractive in a sort of way; I don't exactly know how or why, but I certainly felt an emotional need to get closer to him. I started fantasising about him, as one does, and not that long after I somehow found myself walking into his bedroom naked and boldly getting into bed with him, something I couldn't have imagined in my wildest dreams a few months before.

If he'd been able to resist that, I'd have been totally shattered, but there was no problem. It couldn't have been much different if he'd been expecting me, and perhaps he had: certainly I got the feeling he wanted it as much as I did. Not only that, whereas during the day he was of course the boss, in bed I was the dominant one, and he followed my lead all the way as if to the manner born. Yet when he came down to breakfast the next morning, there was not the faintest acknowledgement of what had happened the night before, and though my going to him became a pretty regular thing two or three nights each week, and he never resisted any of my demands, his behaviour to me during the rest of the day didn't change; he was as reserved and withdrawn as ever.

Our coupling, too, was always silent, at least as far as actual words were concerned: sometime I did manage to elicit a gasp or a moan out of him, but though it was plain from the feel of his body that he was really turned on by these nocturnal activities, he was always holding something back. Even when, as most of the time, I gave it my best shot, and did everything I knew of or could invent to get him carried away, he retained this distance between us. But the sex was more satisfying than any I had with my casual pick-ups, which confirmed to me that there was really some bond between us. Even so, I had to admit defeat: there was nothing more I could think of that I could do to break down his reserve.

But then, a few months after I'd started these nocturnal visits, I did get a sort of acknowledgement: he added another key to my key-ring, and though he said absolutely nothing about it, I guessed it must be the key to the locked door in the cellar. Of course the very next day, as soon as he'd gone off to wherever he went, I couldn't resist having a look inside, but there wasn't very much to see at all, for in fact my key only opened the way to another small room, done up in the same mixture of blues, and having on its far side another door, also locked, but painted pink, which this second key wouldn't open.

It was obvious he was trying to rouse my curiosity, and of course he succeeded: I was dying to know what was on the other side of that door. So that same evening, at supper, I asked him how many rooms there were in the cellar, and he answered that there were seven.

'Do I get to see them?' I asked, and then he told me that to get the key to each room I had to spend a night in the preceding one. With just the tiniest flicker of a smile, he added that I had already got through the white room. At the time I didn't understand what he meant, but I certainly was dead curious to know what the whole schemozzle was about. Already, though, I suspected something at least slightly murky, so that I didn't know at that stage whether I'd want to take up what was obviously some kind of test or challenge.

I didn't say anything one way or the other at the time, and he didn't press me. I mulled it over for a few days, but in the end I wanted too much to know what it was all about. I suspected that at the very least it might give me a better understanding of what Bertram, as he was called — not a name I could bring myself to use, while a more matey term such as Bert was unthinkable — was about, perhaps even help to establish a closer relationship with him. So I suppose I knew from the beginning that I would have to go through with it, even though I didn't entirely relish the prospect. And a few evenings later, at supper, I said to him I wanted to have a try at getting the key of that second door.

So the next night, as he'd instructed me, I stripped off in the antechamber, and then went into the Blue room, which was done up with considerable skill in a progression from lighter shades to darker ones. He was already down there, wearing only one of those head-masks, with slits for the eyes and mouth, and leather cuffs on his wrists and ankles. Though I had no intention of entering into the spirit of what I thought was a ridiculous charade, I had to admit to myself that he really did look rather sexy.

Anyway, it wasn't as difficult as I'd expected, I had to suck him, and then he fucked me, for a surprisingly long time. Though of course I wasn't a virgin in that area by then, I'm much happier when the roles are reversed, so I didn't find it startlingly exciting, and I don't believe he did either. But anyway it passed off well enough, and I hoped, though not very optimistically, that the rest of the rooms would prove no more of an effort.

As we left the room he gave me the key to the next door, but I didn't use it then; I thought I'd rather wait till he'd gone out. When I did go down there again, I found a similar room, only this time done up in pink — a colour I particularly loathe, though that's neither here nor there. The walls were stacked high with dildos of all shapes and sizes, and I guessed then that he was using the colour codes, but to be sure I phoned up the Switchboard.

When I finally got through, the guy on the other end of the phone first of all confirmed my assumption, and then obligingly went thorough the whole list for me — there were over a couple of dozen different ones, if you please, most of them, I hoped, unlikely to apply to any of the seven rooms.

I gave it a rest for a few days, but finally I spent a night in this next room, and to be fair he didn't go mad and try anything totally unreasonable. With due consideration for my lack of experience, he started off with the smallest he had, and though by the end of the session he had graduated to an instrument rather larger than I would have believed I could handle, there were plenty of others that he never got round to, both longer and thicker, which made me quail just to look at them. So though the session went a lot further than I would have preferred, I survived intact, only knackered, and when he finally let me out, I just crawled into bed and had a good sleep.

I took a full week off after that, to give my body time to recover, and during that time mulled over what I was getting into. For the first time I remembered that I had told him I had severed contact with my family, and when I thought about it now I wondered if that was why I'd been chosen, for I couldn't believe mine was the only reply he'd received. If anything happened to me, who was there to bother?

It did seem a bit suspicious, and the next room was grey, which meant he would have me totally helpless. I hummed and hawed, but finally I decided to trust that at the very least he'd want to complete the series, so to speak. In the event, it was no big deal: I had to let him tie me to some sort of contraption. Being completely restrained was a slightly strange sensation, but there was nothing much else to it. He slapped me around a bit, which gave me a sort of mild frisson, but apart from that it was fairly boring, and I got through it by practising relaxation techniques. I had to stay like that all night, and I imagine it could get to you after a while if you let it, but I refused to allow my imagination any rein, and even managed to sleep a fair bit.

However, I was a lot less sanguine about going any further, since the next door was in black — not the blackest black I'd ever seen by any means, from which I drew some small comfort, but still not a colour I'd have chosen for myself. I've never been able to understand what the S&M fraternity get out of their practices: certainly the idea of either inflicting pain or, even worse, having it inflicted, does absolutely nothing for me, and of course I had no idea how far he'd want to go.

By this time I was certain there was something between us. He no longer tried to pretend he didn't welcome our regular sex, responding to everything I did with abandon. Of course, he could have the sort of kinky personality could go from that to committing murder, but I couldn't believe it: I was certain there was some other explanation for his behaviour.

So I finally screwed up my courage and opened the door, when it didn't look too sinister, more trappings than reality. As by this time I felt I'd gone too far to draw back, I had a word with a pub acquaintance who was much more versed in such things than I was, and he suggested something he called a snowball, which apparently is the slang term for a mixture of heroin and cocaine: the heroin to dull my nerves, and the cocaine to prevent me from appearing too torpid and thus giving the game away — for I had no idea whether Bertram would regard what I was going to do as cheating, and I could hardly ask him.

I did as this guy advised, paying a quite extortionate sum for the stuff, and I suppose it did help me to get through it. It wasn't so much that I couldn't feel the physical sensations, as that they didn't bother me very much, to the extent that they could almost have been happening to someone else. Unfortunately, even so I was too tense and, I suppose, too scared, to appreciate the ridiculous aspects of the situation: this masked figure, in black leather shorts with studded wristbands, first of all tying my wrists to a couple of hooks set in the wall and paddling me with a tawse, during which operation, I was relieved to find, he seemed more interested in the domination aspect than actually whacking me hard, Then he applied clothes-pegs and clamps to my spread-eagled body, which was rather more uncomfortable, though he did help me to get through it with liberal sniffs from the poppers bottle. There was some more paddling before it was finally over, but nothing I couldn't cope with, so that it wasn't too bad, but nonetheless I was very relieved when it was all over.

The exit door was red, and though I felt that, after the night I'd just been through, I should be able to cope with it, I was in no hurry, since once again it was something that I had no experience of: indeed, I'd found the idea far too extreme for it ever to interest me.

So it was over a week later that I finally ventured. There was a sling attached to the walls, which strapped me into, and as with the dildos, at least he knew

133

what he was doing: he took everything very slowly, and I suppose probably made it about as easy for me as he could. And eventually, after what seemed like several hours, though I've no idea how long it actually was, and with the help of more poppers than I'd normally use in a week of sex, he did get his hand in, by which time I was limp with exhaustion, because, though he kept telling me to relax, I found it very difficult.

I think the main problem was that even though some of the actual physical sensations, especially at the beginning, weren't too bad, in fact sometimes quite pleasurable, I don't really like the feeling of being the passive partner, and so spent most of my energy in trying to force myself not to fight it.

To my dismay, that wasn't enough for him: I had to return the next night so that he could go a bit further. This time, though, I was more able to relax, eventually even sort of enjoying it, though I thought, when it was all over, that it was just as well I was mainly active, cos I wasn't sure if I'd be able to appreciate a cock after that.

The door to the last room was done in a deep black, so I anticipated the worst, and when I unlocked it and looked inside, I really did pause to consider if I was prepared to go through with it. There were a number of positively gothic pieces of apparatus lining the walls, and to put it mildly, I didn't fancy any of them in the tiniest bit, while the thought that I might possibly have to experience the lot was frankly slightly terrifying.

Once again I asked myself whether I trusted Bertram enough to put myself unreservedly in his hands. All this performance had demonstrated quite clearly, if I hadn't realised it before, that there was something pretty strange in his make-up, and I didn't want to end up a statistic.

I was no nearer understanding him than I had been when I first met him, and I could only make vague guesses as to what all the rigmarole was about. So it was nearly a month before I could nerve myself, but finally I decided that, having got that far, I had to go ahead. I got a stronger snowball, and even that wasn't enough to prevent the night being the most unpleasant I've ever spent, or hope to. Fortunately he seemed, as before, more interested in domination than torture.

To start off, with the use of a pair of manacles, something that looked to me like a dog-collar, and a colourful collection of chains, he fixed me up in a sort of hog-tie, and then pushed my helpless body around while slapping me. I was, to be honest, too frightened to get mad at this, so I forced myself to relax, telling myself that at least it was better than him actually using any of the various implements hanging on the wall.

Unfortunately that was just the hors-d'oeuvres. During the course of the night I had to experience most of the pieces of apparatus, and at times I felt like pinching myself to make sure I wasn't dreaming, except that it was being done for me: certainly a few months before, if anyone had said I'd find myself in a cellar fixed to a rack, with someone dropping hot candle-wax on my naked body I' d have though they were mad.

More than once I felt like begging him to stop, but I held out, mostly because I had to make everything else I'd been through worthwhile. The session finally ended with me, with my hands tied behind my back, wearing a couple of nipple-clamps which by then were really beginning to make their presence felt, and with some complicated contraption round my genitals which was pretty uncomfortable, on my knees in front of him sucking him off while he slapped me occasionally, more decoratively than seriously, thank god, with some sort of leather whip he was holding.

I did my best to bring him off as quickly as possible, as you can well imagine, and by the time he finally came in my mouth, I was feeling more dead than alive. So when I was released, I just grabbed the key, tottered up to my bedroom with my clothes, and went to bed. I will say for him that he certainly knew what he was doing, because when I examined my body in the mirror the next morning, there was hardly a mark to be seen, just a certain amount of redness, and while I was still sore in places, he hadn't actually done any damage at all.

When I eventually saw him again, which wasn't till supper-time, I imagine he was curious to know when I'd be opening the seventh door, but I said nothing about it, and he didn't ask. By now I had a pretty strong suspicion as to what I'd find when I opened it, and I didn't know how I'd handle it if I found what I expected.

So I didn't do anything, just kept the key in my drawer, and after a while it was obvious, though he did his best to hide it, that Bertram was on tenterhooks, waiting for me to use it. But now the next move was up to me, and I wasn't going to be stampeded into a course of action that I might afterwards regret. For one thing, if my worst suspicions were true, I needed to make sure I wasn't thought to have any complicity. The date of my arrival should be a sufficient alibi, I hoped, and then really a more important question was what would happen to me if, for one reason or another, he ceased to be around?

I thought this over for nearly three weeks until I was as sure as I could be that I had chosen the right course of action. Then, one evening, after we'd eaten, I asked if I could have a word, and I told him what I wanted. I believed that he would agree I had earned what I demanded, by having got possession of the seven keys, and sure enough he didn't cavil; he agreed to have documents prepared straightway, one naming me as his heir, and the other giving me power of attorney to control his affairs, should he not be in a position to do it himself.

A few days later he brought the documents to me, properly drawn up and signed, and handed them over without speaking. I read them through in front of him, and then I told him what I intended to do. I would keep the key to the seventh door, but I said I had no intention of using it. Nor would I make it available to anyone else. He looked at me when I said that, and I looked back straight into his eyes, and he knew that his secret was a secret no longer. I think in a way he was relieved to have control taken away from him: I don't push it, but it's quite plain who's in charge now, and he doesn't seem to object. And one of these nights soon, I expect, I'll take him down to the cellar.

A LITTLE CHAT

Mrs. Melchett was sitting in her lounge, waiting. She had switched off the television and taken her curlers out, an indication that there was some serious matter on her mind, which she intended to address as soon as her husband returned. It wasn't long before she heard him putting the key in the lock, after which he came into the lounge and gave her a perfunctory peck.

She stopped him as he was about to go out again. 'George,' she began, 'I think you should have a word with Melvin. He seems to be in need of being spoken to seriously.'

Mr. Melchett, who had long ago realised how little his wife and he really had in common, did his best to avoid the task she had in mind for him, though he well knew it was a forlorn hope. 'I hope he hasn't made another pass at the milkman?' he suggested flippantly.

Virginia ignored his attempt to lighten the atmosphere. 'I don't like the way he's started going around with a man twice his age,' she announced. 'It isn't healthy.'

'O dear,' her spouse said insincerely. 'Has the fellow got this new TB or something?'

Now she had started, she was not going to allow him to deflect her. 'I was referring to his moral health. There are times when even you must start to take a serious view of your responsibilities as a parent.'

George Melchett sighed resignedly. Seating himself in one of the armchairs, and making himself as comfortable as he could — comfort had not been the thought uppermost in Mrs. M's mind when she chose them — he said 'Perhaps you'd better tell me why you think this is one of them.'

It was a source of persistent irritation to her that he looked so much younger than his thirty-eight years, but she brushed it aside for now, and continued rhetorically 'You're not trying to tell me you haven't noticed your son is always going about with this fellow, Colin Something-or-other?'

'Going out with him a few times is hardly a red alert,' George offered pacifically.

'It's much worse than that,' Virginia pronounced magisterially. 'They seem to spend most of their spare time together.'

'I don't really see what you're so worried about,' George complained. 'I believe Colin is a very cultured person, so he's bound to exert a good influence on our son. So far Melvin's cultural activities have been chiefly noticeable by their absence.'

'That's as may be,' Virginia pronounced heavily. 'But why should this cultured person be interested in Melvin?'

'Now you're being too hard on the boy,' George protested. 'I admit he has his rough spots, but after all he has only just turned eighteen. In many ways I think he's quite an attractive young fellow, even though I am his father.'

'That's just the trouble,' Mrs. pounced. 'I strongly suspect that Colin fellow has the same opinion.'

'Well, I should certainly hope so,' Mr. agreed warmly.

Virginia Melchett often had the feeling that she and her husband were conversing through a wall of plate glass, and it was the same now. George never seemed to understand what she was getting at, and obviously at times it was deliberate. But she refused to let it stop her, and with a sigh for his obtuseness, she pointed out 'Then he could have designs on him.'

George's motto had always been 'anything for a quiet life,' the inevitable result being that he usually didn't get it, and so now he resigned himself to having to sort this out before he was allowed to relax with his usual book before bedtime. He explained calmly 'If the poor fellow is going to spend time and effort, not to mention money, on trying to raise our son's cultural level, he's certainly going to need every possible enticement. My worry is that Melvin is too callow and inexperienced to be able to keep him interested.'

'Culture, culture!,' Mrs. exclaimed in tones of deep disgust. 'You're always harping on it. No doubt it's all very well in its place, but not when the price is too high.'

'What price are we talking about?' Mr. asked innocently.

'Leading him into immorality.'

'What on earth are you going on about?' asked George, who, having accepted that the matter would have to be thrashed out, had determined to get what amusement he could out of the argument.

Virginia was unable to prevent a blush suffusing her pale cheeks. 'Letting that Colin have his way with him,' she explained bravely.

'Nonsense,' George exclaimed briskly. 'I'm quite sure Melvin will be getting the best of the bargain. And with any luck he should enjoy Colin's attentions, not to mention all the useful experience.'

'That would be absolutely appalling. Even you can't want him to — well, get a taste for that sort of thing.'

'Why not?' George asked provocatively.

'Because what he needs is to find some nice girl, and settle down and have children,' she declared with as much conviction as she could muster, especially since she knew that George was an agnostic in these matters.

'At eighteen?'

'Well, alright,' she hedged, 'it doesn't have to be Miss Right first off. But at least he ought to have started looking.'

'So you'd rather he was out there screwing the birds than acquiring some culture to enable him to mix in better social circles?'

She was unable to prevent her embarrassment at his coarse way of putting things becoming visible, but nonetheless she said defiantly, 'If the circles consist of men like Colin, then yes I would.'

A door opened on the floor above, and they heard the object of their discussion descend the stairs. When he came into the lounge, they saw he was dressed to go out. She noticed with dismay that he was wearing those ripped jeans again. They were practically indecent, and anyway he had a couple of nearly new pairs; why couldn't he put those on and look less like a tramp? She took some pride in the fact that he certainly was a good-looking boy, much of it from her side, she considered, but he never seemed to want to dress smartly and show himself off to best advantage. However, she knew it was useless her saying anything on the subject; she'd tried often enough before, so she just tightened her lips.

'Hi,' Melvin said casually. 'I'm just off to a disco.'

'At eleven o'clock? What sort of disco?' asked his mother automatically.

'One where they play loud pop music and people dance,' Melvin told her patiently.

'Are you going to dance?' she asked, looking doubtfully at how tightly his jeans moulded themselves around his contours.

'The purpose of my going there is to work off my youthful energy in socially acceptable ways, mother,' Melvin explained. 'Or would you rather I was out on the streets mugging old ladies and vandalising telephones?'

'Are you meeting that Colin there?'

'Of course.'

Virginia turned to her husband. 'I don't see how you can call that improving his cultural level,' she exclaimed with the satisfaction of at last having a valid point to make.

'Colin's only going because I made him,' Melvin explained.

'Why is that?' Mrs. couldn't resist asking.

'I told him that, if I have to go to the Opera with him, then he has to do a bit of slumming with me.'

Virginia's ears pricked up. 'Slumming!' she exclaimed. 'What sort of disco is this, then?'

'All discos are slumming to Colin,' Melvin explained further. 'I have to twist his arm to make him take me.'

'You're not a child any more,' said his mother, who had much preferred him when he was. 'Why can't you go on your own?'

His father was impressed at the patience with which Melvin pointed out to his mother 'Because then he would be deprived of the incredible pleasure of my company. Not to mention that he knows full well I'd leave with somebody else.'

Virginia, one of life's triers, went on to another tack. 'I must confess,' she said, 'I find it difficult to see why a man of his age should want to go around with a boy like you.'

George laughed. Virginia glared at him while Melvin, who had been unable to repress a grin, said 'You might be surprised how many men would like to, Mother. Colin merely happened to be head of the queue.'

'I find it even more difficult to understand why you should want to go around with someone twice your age. Your father gives you a very generous allowance, far too much in my opinion, so you can well afford to pay for your own entertainment.'

'Colin is helping me to fill in all those gaps that you left in my education,' her son told her.

She was immediately on the defensive. 'It's not our fault you didn't want to go to college.'

'Unfortunately the things I'm interested in learning don't seem to be on the curriculum,' Melvin explained. 'Otherwise I'd have signed up like a shot.'

Virginia couldn't leave it alone. 'I suppose Colin is the sort of creature who makes a habit of preying on boys too young to see through his blandishments?' she suggested acidly.

'Virginia, really,' George protested mildly.

'I think the time has come to call a spade a spade,' she announced defiantly.

George had long ago resigned himself to the fact that he had been weak enough to allow their sham of a marriage to continue for reasons which he now felt were insufficiently adequate, but he got some satisfaction out of doing his best to ensure that Melvin should not make the same mistake. Of course Virginia was well aware of the measures he took to make his life tolerable, but neither of them ever mentioned the subject. Suddenly, though, he felt a need to support his son.

'Then you should be sure you've got hold of the right end,' he interposed. 'I asked Colin to take an interest in Melvin.'

Virginia was thunderstruck. 'You! Whatever for?' she demanded.

'So that he should have a better start in life than his father,' George explained. 'Instead of getting married young, and being caught in the treadmill, it would be better for him to spend a bit of time learning about the higher things of life.'

'Judging by the number of times I've found his bedroom door locked,' Virginia protested with a closer approach to reality than she normally allowed herself, 'it seems more like the lower things.'

'You can't blame Colin for that, mother,' Melvin interrupted. 'I'm at my physical peak just now: surely you wouldn't want me to waste it?'

His mother pointed out with dignity 'There is such a thing as self-control.'

'But what would I be controlling it for?' Melvin asked.

A steady diet of romantic fiction had the words ready on his mother's lips. 'When you do decide to get married, you would come to your bride untarnished.'

This was too much for George. 'Come on, Virginia,' he exclaimed heatedly. 'You wouldn't want him to be completely inexperienced, surely? Look at the problems we had.'

'Now is hardly the time or place to go into that, George,' his spouse said frostily. 'In any case, I somehow doubt that the experience he is getting with Colin is the sort that would be of any value to him when he does decided to enter on a legitimate liaison.'

'I think you're wrong there, Virginia,' George explained. 'I made sure Colin was versatile before I introduced him to Melvin.'

Virginia was suitably shocked. 'You introduced him to Melvin! What on earth gave you the idea he was a suitable sort of person for our son?'

'I had known Colin for some time beforehand .'

'And I suppose you said to him "I want someone to teach my son a bit of culture, and while you're about it, you can teach him a few other tricks as well".'

'Actually,' George explained with dignity, 'it started off with Colin offering to perform those services for me.'

'I see it all, now, George.' Virginia was genuinely scandalised. 'I must confess I am appalled. 'No thank you, Colin, but let me introduce you to my son; I think you might fancy him.'

'I take my responsibilities as a father seriously,' George protested, 'whatever you say. I wouldn't have dreamed of introducing Colin to him unless I had proof positive he was what was needed.'

'I sincerely trust I don't understand what you're talking about,' Virginia made a determined attempt to bring the conversation back to safer areas.

George turned to Melvin. 'It was quite a wrench to pass him on to you, son. So I'm glad to see you're making full use of the opportunity.'

'Colin seems to think I make too much use,' Melvin remarked. 'He said he was thinking of asking for an amnesty.'

George smiled. 'At least if you exhaust yourself dancing, you won't be quite so demanding when you get back to his place,' he pointed out.

'Unfortunately he'll be exhausted as well. The music seems to do that to him even without his doing any dancing. Luckily, Steven's going to be there, and I enjoy dancing with him.'

Virginia was unable to repress her womanly curiosity at this hint of amorous complications. 'Doesn't that make Colin somewhat jealous?' she enquired, doing her best to sound as if she wasn't interested in the answer. It was at times like this that she most regretted not having been able to persuade George to give her a second child. By the law of averages, he or she, she wouldn't have minded which, would have been bound to have inherited much more of her characteristics than this one, who was only too clearly his father's son.

Melvin was off at a tangent. 'That gives me an idea. I'll take Dad. He and Colin could sit in the bar and talk over old times, while Steve and I flash our bodies around on the floor, and then he can drop Steven back when we all leave.'

'Your father has better things to do than accompany you to some low haunt,' Virginia proposed with admirable optimism.

'No, I haven't,' George contradicted her enthusiastically. 'I don't think I've met Steven: what's he like?'

'I'm sure you'll get on with him, Dad,' Melvin said encouragingly. 'He's quite a goer.'

Virginia felt she had to make one last attempt to restore normality before things got totally out of hand. 'George! You're not seriously considering ...' she tailed away.

'What proper father would not want to help his son out of a difficult social situation?' George asked rhetorically. 'I consider it my duty to sacrifice a quiet evening of domestic bliss to the noise and glare of some rowdy dance-hall, for the sake of my only son's happiness.'

'You'll have to make yourself presentable before I allow you to accompany us,' Melvin warned. 'Take that ghastly Fair-Isle pullover off, and put on some jeans. Tight ones.'

'Why does he have to wear tight jeans?' Virginia wanted to know.

'He may as well show off what he's got,' Melvin explained.

'What for?' his mother asked, her tone proclaiming she knew she was out of her depth.

'One never knows,' Melvin told her sententiously.

She sighed. 'Things have come to a pretty pass when I have to ask my son to keep an eye on his father. Perhaps I ought to join you, just to make sure he behaves himself in a proper manner.'

'Sorry, mother,' Melvin said. 'Ladies Night is not till Tuesday. Unless you wanted to drag up.'

'I think I'd rather wait till Tuesday,' Virginia remarked coldly. 'Do you mean to say there will be no persons of the feminine gender present to exert a tender softening influence over all these crude expressions of rampant maleness?'

'In that case,' George remarked with unwonted fervour, 'I'm definitely going.'

Virginia could not let that pass without reproof. 'George,' she chided, 'that is not a nice remark after nearly twenty years of wedded bliss.'

'Sorry, dear,' George apologised. 'But twenty years of wedded bliss is just what I'm trying to save Melvin from.'

'Dad, go and change,' Melvin hustled his father. 'You actually look quite good in jeans; I could almost fancy you myself.'

This time Virginia didn't have to pretend to be scandalised. 'Melvin!'

'It's all right, mother,' her son laughed. 'I was only joking. Don't stop up for us: culture takes a long time.'

SO YOU WANT TO BE A DISCIPLE

It's surprisingly easy being a Guru. At least, that's what I've found. I don't intend to suggest that it's possible for any ordinary person such as yourself — I mean, no offence meant, but you know as well as I do that you could never make a Guru in a million years, not if you smeared yourself with yak butter and prostrated yourself at my feet. Though of course I wouldn't let you, because the stuff is distinctly odoriferous, so that, after a brief trial, I have arranged for my disciples to use a vegetable alternative, which each one has to prepare for himself by pounding the seeds of the carioca plant and extracting the oil present. I look on this little discipline as a Western equivalent of yak-milking

What I meant to say was that, once I realised that I had reached the stage of enlightened wisdom where I had discovered the secrets of living and, out of the charitableness of my nature, intimated to a few select souls that I was willing to guide them on their own doubtless rather more tortuous path to whatever lesser heights they might prove capable of achieving, I found the actual process of filling the role of a Guru simplicity itself.

As I said, I was surprised by this at first, but on reflection I realised that, once one has solved the secret of life for oneself, the problems of others are as nothing, and the way forward is blindingly obvious — to one with my clarified vision, that is, not to those ordinary mortals who haven't reached my degree of enlightenment.

I hope I don't sound arrogant, because of course that is one of the things I am totally beyond. But when one knows and understands everything, everything of importance, that is, even though one is in fact humble in oneself because one realises one's insignificant place in the cosmos, one is apt to appear a spot over-sure of oneself to those who haven't yet learnt to look at life from the viewpoint of the Eternal Verities

So I'm sure you won't be offended when I explain that my saying how easy I personally have found it is not an invitation to every Tom, Dick or Harry to set himself up as a Fount of Wisdom. The last thing we need is seekers after truth being led astray by the unsuitably qualified.

You will gather, after my little explanation, that I'm not proposing to make any attempt to train you to become a Guru yourself. For one thing, and I mean this in the nicest possible kind of way, I doubt very much if you've got what it takes. But in spite of the fact that I detect a certain lack of spiritual capacities in you, I am perfectly willing to help you reach whatever slight degree of self-knowledge and comprehension you may possibly be able to attain.

So I thought I'd give you a spot of general information first, just so that you'll get some idea of what becoming one of my disciples involves, and then you can go away, mull it over, and decide if you're capable of the effort and discipline required. But I should warn you that giving up once you've started will probably leave you in a worse state than if you'd never started at all.

The first thing you need to know about Gurus is that we don't care. Not in a heartless way, of course; we're all boundlessly benevolent, and we like to see people leading happy lives, though of course preferably not through mindless involvement in what earlier teachers have memorably characterised as the World, the Flesh, and the Devil. The point is, though, that we are not emotionally involved in the quality of your life.

I rather suspect that you are too caught up in what you think the world has to offer to choose to sit at my feet — speaking metaphorically, of course — but none the less I will give you for free one of the basic keys to understanding this world we live in, even though it took me many years to arrive at it, and it will surely take you many more to properly grasp it. This is that everyone is really doing what they want to do. Of course many of them, probably much the larger majority, are either partially or totally unaware of this fact, but that is of no consequence. The point is that, until one fully understands and accepts this fact about oneself, one is not ready to progress along the path of enlightenment.

I am not going to enter into any sort of discussion about it: either you agree with me or you don't, and no amount of intellectual arguments I put forward in favour of my view will change your mind. In any case, we Gurus don't argue with our disciples; we are not out to prove anything. The delusion that rational argument has any validity in the real world, as opposed to the everyday impermanent succession of appearances that we mis-name reality, is one of the most unfortunate aspects of western thinking.

However, once you have accepted it, and I mean believe it, not just agree intellectually, then you will have reached the starting-point, and I would probably be prepared to take you on. But I should warn you that most fall by the wayside at some point in their progress, and so far as I am concerned that is where they will stay, unless they can sort themselves out and follow my precepts.

My very first disciple was one of these unfortunates. He came to me originally because of his dissatisfaction with his love-life: when I questioned him, he claimed that he had realised its futility, and how emotional attachments were a stumbling-block on the path to wisdom. I suspected, even during the interview, that he had not so much seen through the trap of emotional commitment as been disappointed in his attempts to attain it, but he was my first applicant, so I went against my better judgement, and agreed to take him on.

Needless to say, he was unable to relinquish the longing for this kind of emotion, and so when what appeared a suitable opportunity to try for it again arose — because, as I pointed out to him at the time, he had deliberately left himself open to it — he jumped into it, such little progress as he had made was thrown aside, and he was back where he had been when he started. Unfortunately for him, he still, from time to time, has longings for something more than everyday life, so he is in the unhappy position of not being able to give himself whole-heartedly to either, and is doomed to permanent dissatisfaction until he changes.

It seems to be very difficult for most people to comprehend that the way of complete acceptance can also be the path to transcendence: they are much happier with the notion of renunciation, and this is no doubt due to the misleading effect of the Gnostic heresy, that the soul is good and the flesh evil. I mention this because I expect you will find much of my teaching strange, so that initially you would have considerable difficulty accepting it. But you just have to take my word for it, and if you can't do that, you are not yet ready to become my disciple.

Go away and reflect on what I have said. When you realise that you know absolutely nothing of any use, you have reached the beginning of wisdom, and may apply to me to start you on the path to enlightenment. Bring your own mortar and pestle.

THE TREATMENT

The fact that I'd been expecting it didn't seem to make much difference to the effect it had when I finally knew for certain: I was fairly stunned. All the rest of it, the counselling, the instructions from the doctor, everything hit me as if I was just coming out of an anaesthetic; I heard the words, I even knew what they meant in themselves, but they didn't seem to relate to me.

I suppose, though, that I gave sufficient impression of being compos mentis because, after they'd all done their various routines, they sent me away under my own steam. I wandered out of the hospital and looked for a bus-stop. But after I'd been standing there for a couple of minutes I decided I didn't want to go straight home, and looked around for a cafe or snack-bar. I couldn't see one in my field of vision, so I wandered up the street until I found one.

When I was inside, I got myself a cup of coffee, and sat there sipping it mechanically. I remembered Robert, one of the first in this country to die from it. That must have been about twelve years ago. I couldn't stop myself replaying scenes of him in the hospital. He'd been quite a big guy, but at the last he was reduced to looking like a matchstick.

The thought of ending that way was horrifying, but of course he'd died a long time ago, and the medics had had all that time to improve the treatment. I knew they weren't able to cure me, but at least they could offer me a better quality of life while I — was dying, I had to force myself to end the thought. Confronting it head on like that helped to wake me from my daze: I paid for my coffee, went back into the street, and caught the bus home.

How does one deal with what amounts to a sentence of death? Not very easily, I found. I've been positive so long, without any particular problem I was aware of, that I didn't really bother about it any more. There are quite a lot of guys among my acquaintance who've been positive as long as or longer than me, and who still haven't developed any symptoms of anything to worry about. Up till just recently I'd been including myself among the lucky ones. Now it was an entirely different ball-game. When I got back, I couldn't relax; I wandered around fairly aimlessly, all the time a churning mess of mixed emotions inside, but not knowing what to do to get back some sort of control over what I was feeling.

Eventually I phoned Richard, an ex from my younger days who's a lot older than me, or for that matter the rest of my friends, and told him my news. He sounded genuinely upset, and offered to come straight round. I put him off at first, but he pressed me, and I realised I would like to see him. So I said okay, and he was with me within half-an-hour.

I suppose the physical affection he gave me as soon as he arrived was actually what I most needed, and before very long I was having a good cry on his shoulder, with him encouraging me to let myself go. After that I did feel a bit better. I made us a coffee, he sat with me, and we talked the situation through a bit.

He was a lot more positive than I felt, and even while I appreciated what he was trying to do for me, I was thinking it was all very well for him: he wasn't ill. He was nearly twenty years older than me, and I well knew that he'd been around a good bit in his time, but by the luck of the draw his generation hadn't been exposed to the same sort of risk as mine.

Anyway, he said he knew a guy that had a rather different slant on this business, and wanted me to agree to see him. At first I felt I couldn't be bothered, but then I thought 'What the hell' and said okay, so Richard undertook to arrange for him to phone me. And he did a couple of days later. He was one of those enthusiastic types that I always find a bit exhausting, but I let him come round, with some misgivings, mainly to please Richard.

The fellow was rather as I had expected — I almost said feared. I have to give it him that he did look well, even though, according to Richard, he had been diagnosed the same as me. But then people who have an obsessive interest often do — look well, I mean — and I have idly wondered whether it's because in some way they don't even allow their bodies the time to get ill. Anyway, it's not my style; I like to get my work out of the way and then go out and enjoy myself — or that's what I used to like, things are obviously going to be a bit different, I thought.

He was quite sweet, and I'd probably have given him a second glance if I'd seen him in a pub, but at close quarters, though he was obviously making some effort to contain himself, he was rather overpowering, especially as I was feeling a bit sick, and had already lost the contents of my stomach before he arrived, which of course made me feel weaker than ever. But to be fair, the medics had warned me this was a common side-effect of the stuff they'd given me, so I couldn't really complain. And then this Jimmy turns up, and he has one of those conspiracy theories to explain everything to his own satisfaction, like so many of the world's nutters.

This time it was the medical establishment who were the villains. I suppose I was a bit cool to his opening gambits, cos he was soon trying to blind me with statistics, which he had off pat — the sure sign of a Grade A bore, I thought to myself with a sigh. I listened with rather less than half an ear to the figures he was reeling off about life expectancy, cancer patient survival, and various other matters which I didn't actually find of the most immediate relevance.

Okay, I know what I've got has some similarities to cancer, but it isn't cancer, and with the vast sums that are being spent on trying to find a cure, and the number of top-flight people involved in it, there's bound to be a breakthrough sooner or later. I wasn't going to get myself all stressed up by arguing with him, but of course I could see the holes in what he was trying to tell me at once. When one thinks of the successes of medical research, such as, for instance, antibiotics, insulin, and Valium, none of which we would have without the kind of research he was rubbishing, it was obvious his arguments didn't hold water.

He was so anti-establishment, I suspect not just in that particular matter but in everything, that I soon realised that he'd have opposed what we might call the 'official' line, whatever it was. He argued that practically all great advances have come from people outside the main line, and okay he did have a few examples to support his argument, in fact he rattled off a whole list of them, most of whom I've forgotten, though it included a few names I recognised like John Dalton, the Wright brothers, and Edison. But to the unprejudiced mind, it's quite obvious these are merely the exceptions that prove the rule

I pointed out to him that it's the function of experts to know more about their subject than other people. That is why we pay them, after all, and if they weren't doing their job in a useful way, then we wouldn't be employing them. It was all very well for him to be picking holes in what they were doing, but since by definition they were experts and he wasn't, how could he have sufficient background of knowledge to be able to make such a judgement?

He tried to dodge that argument by saying that he considered the whole basis of their approach to health was wrong, a sweeping statement that practically took my breath away. But I kept my cool, since I'd already realised he was one of those types you could argue with until the moon went blue without changing their mind on anything. I just quietly said that my previous point applied to that as well, and when he started again didn't say any more, just made vague noises, and did my best to look as if I was thinking about what he'd said.

In fact, it soon emerged that what he was trying to sell me was the anti-drug line, and out came more statistics. I had more or less glazed over by then, though when he told me that over thirty per cent of hospital patients suffer unwanted side-effects from drugs, that did strike a bit nearer home, but then, as they say, there's no gain without pain. The last one he tried on me was that one in seven patients in hospital in the United States are there being treated for adverse reactions to drugs. I don't know what he thought he was doing; certainly all this didn't exactly cheer me up. I already knew that the particular drugs I had to take weren't exactly a barrel of fun, and that, because they had to be so strong, they were bound to do a few unpleasant things to me, but there's no rational alternative.

He was obviously too far gone to be able to see it, but the mere fact of the amount of money that was spent on medical research showed how seriously it was being taken, and to imagine that a few tin-pot cranks could have anything to offer besides a sort of faith-healing, for types like him, who are gullible enough to be taken in by their theories, was too ludicrous for words.

But I didn't say this to him, since he was a friend of Richard's, just accepted a load of pamphlets, promised I'd read them carefully, and got rid of him as quickly as I could without being impolite. I took a quick look at them: one of them was all about what vitamins I should take — I mean really it's ridiculous, the medical profession know all about vitamins. They invented them, for goodness' sake, and if they'd do me any good they'd have prescribed them for me already.

Another was about what it called holistic therapy, which seems to involve such things as hypnosis, acupuncture and meditation among others! I've no objection to people playing around with such activities if it keeps them happy, but if this guy seriously imagined that I was going to rely on this sort of fringe idea when my life was on the line, he had another think coming.

I mean, doctors go into the profession because they want to cure people, and if there were a better way of doing it than they've discovered so far, they'd be onto it like a shot. So I stuffed all his leaflets in the bin, and took my next dose of tablets.

THE TRUE STORY

Only a man could ever have been taken in, but the dumb blonde type has always been a good deal more successful than it deserves — how anyone can seriously compare that washed-out look with the lustrous quality of really black hair, not to mention the much better complexion that goes with it, I really can't imagine — and thus I suppose I shouldn't have been so surprised. Certainly those Brothers Grimm were completely landed, hook, line, and sinker, swallowing the whole outrageous pack of lies as if she were a female George Washington, and adding a few more of their own for what one might charitably assume were purely literary reasons — that is if one pays their rag-bag collection the compliment of calling it literature.

I mean, I ask you: a teenage girl living quite unchaperoned in a house with a number of single men is hardly the sort of set-up that anyone with any knowledge at all of the ways of the world would consider entirely innocent. And in fact, though I'm not one to listen to idle gossip, it was common knowledge that what went on there would have made Kraft-Ebbing's eyes pop. But because she had tits the size of melons — though if what I've been told about silicone is true, they won't stay the way they are for ever — and could put on an ingenuous smile, the men were putty in her hands. I spoke to the Chief of Police more than once, but though he always assured me he'd look into it, nothing was ever done. It wouldn't in the least surprise me if he was in the habit of making surreptitious visits there himself, since I know for a fact that his wife flatly refuses to indulge him in some of his more outrageous ideas.

But live and let live, I say, and as long as they remained discreet about what they got up to, and didn't impinge on any of my affairs, I was prepared to more or less turn a blind eye, since I know what men are like, and I've learnt the hard way that, if they aren't getting what they want from one source, they'll go and seek it from another. It was a sort of unspoken truce so far as I was concerned, and it was only when she really got above herself that I was compelled to step in and do something.

Now that my son has reached nineteen, I was worried that he would display the same unfortunate capacity for allowing any nubile female to lead him by the nose that his father had. Of course, once I'd married William, I'd been able to put a stop to most of that, though, even after I did my best to make sure he never got up to anything, he still continued to moon over one after another in a rather pathetic fashion. It obviously behoved me to find a suitable wife for Henry as soon as practicable, but while I was searching in the proper areas for someone who could fit the bill, the wretched boy came across her at some party or other and, like a real chip off the old block, was immediately smitten.

As any good mother would, I'd done my best to keep him from the sort of parties, and places, where he'd be likely to meet that sort of person, but I do have rather a lot of other responsibilities, and every so often he'd manage to evade my vigilance and associate with quite undesirable types. As far as I could gather, from the fairly incoherent account he gave me the next morning, she'd pretended not to know who he was — as if every marriageable female for miles around wouldn't know everything relevant about all the eligible bachelors — and he hadn't said anything about his exalted position to her, charmed by the thought that he was fancied for himself alone, always a good line with gullible males, which I well know is most of them.

Well, I tried reason, though many years' experience of dealing with his father had told me it was almost certainly a lost cause from the outset. I pointed out that the privileges of his position carried with them certain responsibilities, so that it was incumbent upon him, etc. etc. But I might as well have been talking to a statue. He had made up his mind, and he just kept repeating that she was the only girl who'd ever really appealed to him; if he couldn't have her he would rather do without completely. He even hinted that he might indulge another side of his nature, one which certainly was unlikely to produce a son and heir.

As he was my only child, he rather had me over a barrel there, but of course I didn't let him think that; I just temporised and said we'd have to see. In practice this meant that, although I was as usual extremely busy attending to all sorts of matters that didn't just run themselves, though from his attitude you'd have imagined they did, I'd have to go and suss out the position for myself. Of course there was no way I could afford to turn up in person, which would have had to be some sort of official visit, so one night, quite late, I got one of my maids to disguise me. I must say she made an excellent job of it, I looked at least twenty years older, while she had cunningly hidden all those features which give my face its usual classical perfection, not to mention dirtying up my raven locks, which as everyone knows are my crowning glory.

So off I trotted. Because I didn't want anyone to know about what I was doing, I had to make my own way there, which was a bit of a drag. So I wasn't entirely acting when I knocked on the door, pretended I was faint, and asked if they could let me have a glass of water. They invited me in, giving me a chair to sit on, while one of them went off to get a glass, so that I had a chance to look over the set-up.

I'd gone to the kitchen door, of course, which gave me the opportunity to see back-stage, so to speak. Well, I've been around; in my position one gets to learn a lot about the less savoury sides of human nature, but even so, I was frankly appalled. For a start, there was this obvious half-wit, though I believe nowadays we're supposed to call them educationally subnormal, who was wandering around in a permanent state of half-undress and full arousal. Madam was obviously used to it, because she didn't turn a hair when he came up to her clutching himself. She just chided him with 'You know I'm looking after Happy today, Dopey; you must just wait your turn.'

I gathered from this that the seven of them — and a more ill-favoured collection you never saw, not one of them over five foot two, and quite grotesque with it — each had their own day of the week when they got special attention from the lady of the house. In fact, I heard later, from one of my ladies-in-waiting, whose maid knows everything that goes on locally, that the reason the one called Grumpy got his name — they all have these ridiculous nicknames, they don't seem to have proper patronymics like ordinary people — is because his day is Sunday, and so far as she's concerned, it's a day of rest. And, again according to the same source, that's quite deliberate on her part, because even she can't cope with his little peculiarities, which I'm led to believe are both physiological and pathological.

As for the one called Happy! Well, maybe he has got something to be happy about, but I do think he could avoid calling attention to his condition quite so blatantly. One thing's for sure, he doesn't get his trousers off the peg. I was so taken aback I must have looked a spot ill or something, because another of them came up to me. He was carrying a little black bag, and while I watched, half-hypnotised, he opened it, took out a hypodermic syringe, and before I knew what happening he said soothingly 'Now don't you worry, my dear,' and stuck it in my arm.

I gave an enormous yell, as you can imagine, and then I felt quite dizzy. I broke out into a sort of warm sweat, and really the next few minutes are a bit of a blur in my memory. But when I recovered my senses, I tightened my garments, which had unaccountably become rather loose, and, thanking them for their kindness, staggered out and made my way home.

For some reason I felt absolutely shattered, so I wasn't up to doing the whole journey on my own. I had to get my maid to come for me in a carriage, all very embarrassing, because of course I couldn't let anyone else know who I really was, or what I'd been doing. However, eventually I got home, and had a long soak in a hot bath. I tried out a new bath-essence, specially put together for me by the Court Beautician, 'Black Snow-drop,' and it certainly revived me, a process completed by a treatment from one of my Masseurs-In-Waiting — this time it was Number Three, the black one.

By midday the next morning, I felt practically back to my normal self, and I realised something must be done immediately. No way could I possibly allow my poor son, a babe in arms compared to her, to continue in this entanglement. It was a time for stern measures, but of course I had to act covertly, for I knew he would never forgive me if he found out that I was responsible for the operation I was planning.

I summoned the Court Physician, and put the position to him, when it didn't take him long to come up with the perfect solution. So a few days later, I got dolled up again in the same disguise, and went back to their abode. I had with me a basket of apples, all of which had been carefully doctored. This might seem like overkill, but I couldn't leave anything to chance. I needed to ensure that she ate one of them, and that meant that there had to be enough for the whole grisly collection if need be.

I presented them with the basketful 'for being so kind to an old woman' and they thanked me and accepted them. So then I had to just endure the wait, on tenterhooks to see if they had done the job. Of course, there was no way I could easily find out through official channels. Fortunately I have this tame lap-dog at court who dotes on me, a feeling which, I need hardly tell you, is not reciprocated. But he does come in handy when there's one of these awkward little jobs to be done, so I sweetened him up beforehand by inviting him to dance with me before dinner the next evening.

The bandmaster, Wolfgang Something-or other, had the temerity to strike up a popular waltz, 'Nights Of Gladness,' when we swept onto the floor. I gritted my teeth and managed to smile, though of course inside I was regretting the good old days, when he would have been whipped for his insolence.

Anyway, I dutifully followed through with Marmaduke, and I can't complain; I've known it a lot worse. Then I sent him off in the small hours to scout around, and he came back with good news: it seemed all of them were right out.

Once I knew that the way was clear, I ordered a squad down there immediately. Sure enough, they found them all unconscious, and so were able to bring them away without causing undue commotion The one who'd given me the injection had presumably been greedy and eaten a couple or more of the apples, because he proved to have popped his clogs, as the peasants say. I wasn't too upset at this, especially as I've heard since my visit that he was actually a defrocked gynaecologist. There were still six left, so I arranged to have them shipped off to a travelling circus, where they (mostly) settled down quite happily, after some much-needed discipline, and a few months of training.

Her I sent to a House in Buenos Aires where, to nobody's surprise, she proved a great success, soon becoming the *Specialité de la Maison*. I assume she liked it well enough: at any rate, she's never been back here to bother me.

That left me with a couple of problems, which I solved with my usual efficiency. First off, I produced a lad I'd been saving for this sort of emergency, made him Groom of the Bedchamber, and gave him to Henry. As the new arrival had passed the tape-measure test with flying colours, and in addition had been thoroughly instructed in his duties, Henry was so grateful he was practically putty in my hands, and I was able to arrange a politically useful match with no trouble.

Luckily she was a sensible girl with a good understanding of the role of expediency in the governing process, so I was able to arrange for her to go platinum. This was both to keep him sweet, and so that the idiot populace could be fed the sort of romantic mish-mash about love at first sight that these fictioneeers cook up out of their immature fantasy-worlds. She proved a great help to me in running things, while, once Henry understood that all we really needed off him was an heir, or preferably a couple, and some public appearances, while the rest of the time his private life could remain private as far as we were concerned, everything was hunky-dory, and he completely forgot his ridiculous infatuation.

So eventually, as in all the best tales, everyone lived happily ever after. The mine? Oh, I nationalised it, of course: that way the whole kingdom would benefit rather than a bunch of depraved grotesques. I did mean to have them compensated, but it seemed that, by the time the Exchequer was ready to deal with it, the excitements of circus life had proved too much for them.